THE COWBOY DOCTOR

A RODEO ROMEOS ROMANCE

LEAH VALE

Enjoy!
Leah Vale

TULE
PUBLISHING

The Cowboy Doctor

DEDICATION

For my boys, Jake and Luke.
And Terri Reed, for always being there.

CHAPTER ONE

"SAY IT. I'M not doing squat until you say it. I know you want to," a woman's voice said.

"I double-dog dare you," another woman promptly replied with the childish taunt.

Because it was so early in the day and hours before the official Tuesday start of the rodeo, Drew Neisson paused next to the second bucking chute gate at the High Desert Rodeo arena. He looked up, squinting against the bright early June sun to the catwalk above the eight chutes to see who'd just issued what was the ultimate challenge among the Neisson siblings.

He didn't recognize either of the twenty-something women straddling the railing above the bucking chute currently occupied by one of his grandfather's bulls. He definitely would have remembered the lanky blonde who'd issued the dare and the petite redhead sporting a very satisfied smile on her beautiful face if he had met them before.

His not knowing the women was unusual, especially considering they were both obviously competitors of some sort judging by their well-worn leather chaps, scuffed cowboy boots, pristine cowboy hats with shiny long hair curling beneath, and corporate logo-covered western-style shirts. Not only had Drew spent his life in and around Pineville, Oregon, but working as part of the sports medicine team that served the local circuit pretty much guaranteed that he'd at least met if not treated everyone connected to the rodeo around these parts.

No way would he have forgotten the pretty redhead. The *very* pretty redhead who, judging from the belligerent set of her jaw, was seriously considering picking up the gauntlet her friend just threw down.

The redhead glanced down at the bull as if taking its measure. "Double-dog dare?"

"Yep. Double-dog dare," the blonde confirmed with a grin. Maybe they weren't friends. Any dare involving a bucking bull at the rodeo grounds generally didn't end well, even for seasoned bull riders.

"Guess I have to, then." The redhead did not sound upset about whatever she'd just been dared to do. She lifted herself up off the metal railing and swung her leg over the rail to stand on a lower rail *inside* the chute. Then, without a moment's hesitation, she stretched a leg over the bull, catching her booted toes on a gate rail, and commenced easing herself down onto the huge animal's twitching, dust covered back.

Drew's stomach dropped to the arena dirt at the realization of what the clearly foolish woman was about to do. He grabbed the nearest gate rail and hoisted himself up.

"Hey!" he shouted to stop her.

The redhead froze just inches above her intended seat.

As if sensing he was about to go to work, the bull Drew now recognized as Red Rum began surging forward and raking his formidable horns along the chute railing not far from Drew's hands. The ominous sound of horn on metal set dread to churning in Drew's gut.

He dared to take his eyes off the blunted but no less dangerous horns to look into the redhead's striking light hazel eyes—and promptly lost his train of thought. Then Red Rum blew out a wet snort and rattled the gate Drew was standing on as if to remind him.

Drew sent the woman his best scowl. "What do you think you're doing?"

The brim of her light brown felt cowboy hat went up with her raised brows. "What does it look like I'm doing?"

"Something very, very stupid, that's what," Drew shot back. It was hard enough to put these thrill-seekers back together after they'd competed, let alone when they were just goofing around. Didn't she know the damage a bull like Red Rum could cause? The sort of damage that took a life. Sometimes in slow, agonizing ways that he would never wish on anyone. Especially after having had to watch his own mother go through it.

"Stupid because I'm a girl?" she challenged with a hefty dose of attitude.

Despite her petite frame, she was no girl, he thought inanely. She was all woman. And her obvious gender had nothing to do with his objection. His own sister had trained as a bull fighter before she and her husband Bodie started their family.

Forcing his gaze back up to the redhead, Drew countered, "Stupid because you have no bucking rope, gloves, safety vest, or helmet to protect that pretty face of yours."

The blonde giggled. "And she racks up another one who thinks she's pretty."

She wasn't pretty. She was beautiful. And she needed to get away from Red Rum, who was growing more agitated by the minute, which only added to Drew's concern.

The redhead huffed out a breath but inched her shapely backside lower. "Unless you were planning on pulling the gate for me, I wasn't going to actually ride him. He won't even notice little ol' me on his back."

"Trust me, Red Rum will notice." The Wright Ranch bucking bulls were bred to notice a fly on their back and to buck until they'd bucked themselves out for the sheer joy of it.

"Red Rum?" She laughed. "What a great name for this big fella." She let go of the top rail with one hand to reach down and pat the bull's reddish hide. "Me taking a quick seat won't do any harm."

Drew shook his head at her foolishness. He had seen his share of bull riders terribly injured before they'd even left the chute, crushed against the side railings or stacked up into the pass-through gate at the front of the chute. It only took a fraction of a second to end up with broken arms and legs, busted up knees, and twisted ankles. Injuries that could cripple and destroy a career. Take a life.

He reached a hand toward her to coax her out of the

chute like he would a calf tangled in a fence. "I'm sure Red Rum's stock contractor will have a different opinion."

Speaking of which, where were his brothers? Or at the very least his grandfather's men? Someone had to have sent Red Rum into the chute. And he didn't have the time for this sort of foolishness. He was supposed to have been back at the sports medicine trailer ten minutes ago. Since he hoped to take over the program at the end of his sports medicine fellowship, not showing up on time was unacceptable. Impatience and frustration tightened the muscles in his shoulders.

As if on cue, his youngest brother Alec stepped on the rail next to him. "What do we have going here?"

Drew dropped his offered hand that the redhead had pointedly ignored and glanced at his brother. "You tell me. Who sent Red Rum through the chutes from the holding corral?"

"I did. I was going to take a practice ride on him." Alec adjusted the bucking rope slung over his shoulder as if in punctuation. "But I couldn't find Ian to pull the flank strap for me. Have you seen him?"

"No, I haven't. I—"

Red Rum snorted and clanged a horn against the gate railing, yanking Drew's attention back to the chute just in time to see the redhead raise herself back up and off the bull's back. "Hey!"

"Ha! I did it!" she exclaimed as she clambered out of the chute and back onto the catwalk. "I double-dog did it. You owe me now, Sammie."

"What the—" Alec started, then pointed at the women. "Wait, you two must be with that TV show filming the exhibition rides this week."

The blonde, Sammie, planted her hands on the top rail and leaned forward toward them with seemingly no regard for the increasingly agitated bull below her but with full knowledge that the top of her western-style shirt gaped while the rhinestone buttons glinted in the morning sunlight. "That's right. We're stars of *Buckin' TV*," she said with a cheeky smile.

"I wouldn't say stars..." the redhead interjected, brushing the bull dust off her backside and adjusting her chaps.

Drew pulled his gaze from the women to frown at his brother. "What?"

Alec blew out an exasperated breath. "Geez, Drew. Don't you pay attention to anything besides your medical books? These are a couple of the Buckin' Babes—no offense meant, ladies."

"None taken." Sammie winked at him. "Do you want an autograph?"

Alec's grin widened, and he shifted to rest an elbow on a gate railing, appearing as oblivious to the bull as Sammie was. "You know I do." To Drew, he said, "It's quality reality TV, let me tell you. They compete on saddle broncs."

"Ranch saddle broncs," the redhead corrected.

Alec waved her off. "Close enough. Anyway, they're here to do exhibition rides at select rodeos because they normally only get to compete on one circuit down in Texas. Right?" he asked the women, who nodded in confirmation.

"A TV show?" Drew eyed the women again. They were certainly pretty enough to be featured on a reality television show.

Sammie grinned wide while the redhead heaved a sigh and looked up at the clear blue sky.

As if responding to their own cue, a cameraman shouldering what appeared to be a large professional camera, a sound guy with a fuzzy boom mic, and a very harried looking, dark-haired woman hurried along the catwalk.

"What are you two doing now?" the woman asked, recrimination fairly dripping from her tone and expression.

"Nat!" Sammie exclaimed. "You should have seen it. This badass rode a bull!"

The redhead raised both hands and shook her head. "I just sat—"

Nat abruptly stopped, her mouth dropping open briefly before she exclaimed, "What? How many times have I told you not to do anything awesome without us rolling?" She put her fingertips briefly to her temples. "You two are killing me. Quick, do it again!" She grabbed the cameraman and shoved him forward then began positioning the sound man.

She must be the producer or something, Drew thought, and apparently believed beautiful women being maimed or killed by bulls made for good TV.

"No!" Drew and Alec shouted at the same time, making Red Rum stomp his hooves and toss his massive head, sending snot and slobber everywhere.

Nat planted a hand on her black jeans-covered hip and glared down at them. "Excuse me? Who, exactly, are you?"

"Pretty much the owners of this bull," Drew said.

The redhead raised her coppery brows at him again. "Pretty much?"

Alec said, "Our grandfather is Thomas Wright."

The two cowgirls gave simultaneous silent "ohs," but while the redhead shifted her attention to Red Rum and seemed to consider him with new respect, Sammie ran her gaze over Drew and Alec with clear feminine speculation.

Nat looked between them. "Who is Thomas Wright?"

Without taking her eyes off Alec, Sammie answered, "Someone we can't afford to piss off." To her petite friend, she stage whispered, "The good looks, broad shoulders, blond hair, and blue eyes are a definite tip-off."

The redhead shushed her with a wave of her delicate hand.

"Why, exactly, can't we afford to piss this Thomas Wright off?" Nat asked.

The redhead answered, "Because he owns the best bucking broncs on this circuit."

"On any circuit," Sammie added.

The petite cowgirl nodded. "I'd give anything for the chance to ride a Wright Ranch bronc." Her hazel gaze flicked to Drew.

He resisted the urge to dash her hopes with a quick shake of his head when his gaze caught on her bright hazel eyes. His stomach contracted with something hot and intense.

But it didn't change the facts. While their grandfather technically owned all the Wright Ranch rough stock contracted to various rodeos, Drew's second oldest brother Liam was in charge of the bucking broncs. Drew seriously doubted Liam would allow any of his horses to be used in a women's exhibition. Not because the riders would be women, but because the broncs were so rank, and the Wright Ranch didn't need to be known as the contractor who injured or, God forbid, killed a reality TV personality. Though Drew could be wrong. Liam had mellowed remarkably since his marriage to their neighbor Amanda.

The redhead narrowed her eyes at him as if she could read his thoughts, and Drew had to resist the subsequent urge to squirm. He was saved by the producer waving at the girls and her crew as if herding them.

"Come along, kids," Nat said. "Since we have to put that down as a lost opportunity, let's go get some shots of you girls readying your bucking saddles."

Despite already being late for his shift in the sports medicine trailer, Drew hesitated to leave. The little redhead was subtly resisting the producer's attempts to shepherd her toward the stairs leading down from the bucking chute catwalk and loitering in a way that made Drew nervous. He couldn't just leave if she was entertaining thoughts of sitting on Red Rum again.

Alec said, "Go ahead and go. I'll make sure she doesn't try anything."

Drew looked from the redhead to his brother, then to the snorting, agitated bull. "Are you still going to take a practice ride?"

"Not on this guy. I chose life."

Drew let out the breath he hadn't realized he'd been

holding. His little brother deciding to become a professional bull rider had been rough on him. But luckily, Alec had enlisted the help of Bodie Hadley, a former top bull rider who knew from firsthand experience how dangerous bucking bulls could be.

"Don't worry, Drew. You don't have to save me from myself today." Alec looked up toward the end of the catwalk where the two cowgirls were still lingering. "And while I agree you absolutely did the right thing stopping their shenanigans, you do know you can't save everyone, right?"

Drew rolled his eyes at his little brother, but as he turned and walked away, the only thought he had was *I can try.*

"YOU KNOW, YOU could land that cold fish in a heartbeat if you just slowed down enough to try."

With a start, Peyton Halliday yanked her gaze from the cowboy-perfect, jeans-clad backside she'd unwittingly been staring at and met her friend's knowing smirk. She opened her mouth to object, but the only thing she could truthfully object to was said fish being described as cold. There'd been more than a little heat behind those pale blue eyes. And there was no doubting the strength of his shoulders moving easily beneath his crisply pressed black shirt.

Instead, she said, "You know I could never slow down, Sammie. It just wouldn't be livin' to me."

"If you ain't livin', you dying?"

"Exactly." Peyton grinned up at her fellow bronc rider.

Their friendship had steadily—and unexpectedly—grown since Peyton had joined the reality TV show after Natalie's fellow producers had learned of Peyton's past and added her to the cast despite her lack of experience on the women's Texas circuit. Samantha never told Peyton to take it easy or to be careful, and not for the same reasons as the *Buckin' TV* people refrained. Sammie seemed to get Peyton's need for the adrenaline rushes riding broncs gave her as well as the exhilarating flush of freedom her off-time pursuits offered.

Thus, the double-dog dare.

Peyton looked back toward the end of the arena where a certain decidedly hot cowboy was still marching his way out. She definitely didn't appreciate him getting in the way of what would have been an amazing rush from sitting on the back of a real-life bucking bull for more than just a brief second. A Wright Ranch bucking bull, no less.

She shifted her attention to where the other Wright grandson was opening the forward chute gates to send Red Rum through to the holding pen. Peyton released as much of her disappointment as she could on an expelled breath.

Hooking her thumbs into the top of her chaps, she told Sammie, "I'll just have to keep my fingers crossed that I end up drawing the rankest bronc this cute but no less Podunk little rodeo has to offer."

"I'm sure most of the girls will trade with you if need be. Not everyone is looking for the wildest ride they can get."

"Like you?"

"Damn straight. At least inside the arena." Sammie snorted out a laugh, her gaze straying to the younger Wright grandson with a decidedly predatory gleam in her eyes.

Peyton rolled her eyes, turned, and headed for the stairs leading down from the raised metal walkway above the chutes. "You're such a big talker."

"And you don't talk enough, missy," Sammie retorted as she followed Peyton. Their heavy leather chaps, highly decorated for the benefit of the cameras that followed them as much as possible, made descending stairs slow going.

Once down the stairs, Sammie's longer legs had her drawing even with Peyton in two steps. "One of these days you're going to finally kiss and tell, Peyton."

She'd actually have to kiss first, Peyton silently mused. But that would, as Sammie said, take slowing down first.

Something Peyton wasn't willing to do. No way, no how.

CHAPTER TWO

A S HE LEFT the rodeo arena, Drew fought the urge to look back over his shoulder to make sure the Buckin' Babes had indeed left the catwalk above the bucking chutes. He needed to trust Alec to see that Red Rum was safely sent through to the holding pen, unridden. And he did trust Alec. Ever since he'd begun his career as a competitive bull rider, the youngest of the Neisson siblings had shown a newfound maturity. A maturity that had no doubt contributed to Alec's success so far.

Drew determinedly headed through the exit gate left open for the competitors taking advantage of the time between the slack competitions and the highlighted nightly rodeo to practice or just warm up. Before he turned toward where the sports medicine custom fifth wheel was parked though, he glanced back at the catwalk. A near lifetime of worrying about the welfare of others was a hard habit to break. Not that he had any intention of breaking it. Thankfully, the two cowgirls were making their way to the stairs leading down from the catwalk, and their camera crew was nowhere to be seen. Alec was in the process of encouraging Red Rum to pass through the chutes toward the holding pen.

Drew blew out a breath and willed his shoulders to relax. Something he doubted he'd achieve until he made it to the sports medicine trailer where he was already supposed to be, unpacking and putting away supplies.

He picked up his pace to a jog as he neared the vibrant red trailer with the words Rodeo Sports Medicine in bold black lettering and white accents. Once he reached the trailer, he'd finish the restocking of the medical supplies that he'd been in the midst of doing when he'd been interrupted by a call for help from a cowboy with his foot stuck through his stirrup and his ankle twisted. It had been easier for Drew to go to the arena than for them to carry the injured cowboy and his attached saddle to the trailer. Drew had assumed he'd be back and be able to finish restocking before his boss arrived. Thanks to the unexpected Buckin' Babes delay, he was definitely pushing it.

Drew vaulted up the steps to the side door and burst into the trailer that was custom fitted to serve as a mobile medical clinic. Pulled by a matching dually truck, they took it to the rodeos in the circuit they had contracts with throughout the spring to fall seasons.

Dr. Steven Tracer, orthopedic surgeon and Drew's supervising physician, was standing at the supply cabinet restocking the chemical ice packs they seemed to go through like saddle oil and looking more like a cowhand than one of the best bone docs in the region. Drew smiled. Old Doc Tracer wouldn't be old Doc Tracer without his Wranglers, stripped flannel shirt, and beat-up tan cowboy hat.

Doc Tracer and Drew's grandfather had begun their perspective careers at the same time, coming up through the rodeo circuit together. Thomas Wright provided the rodeo rough stock that broke the cowboys, and Doc put them back together again. As soon as Drew made known his desire to go into medicine, his grandfather had introduced Drew to Doc Tracer. And now Drew hoped to take over the running of the Rodeo Sports Medicine program from the older physician so the man could finally retire.

The last thing Doc should be doing was restocking ice packs, Drew thought. Yanking his cowboy hat from his head, he rushed forward, skirting the exam table where he dropped his hat. "I've got that, Doc."

Doc Tracer waved him off. "I'm not so old and infirm I can't bend at the waist and lift ice packs out of a box."

"I know full well you are a country mile from infirm. I saw you the other day at the ranch trying out one of Ian and Jessie's cutting horses."

"That pretty sister-in-law of yours sure knows how to train a good cutter."

"She does, doesn't she?" Drew reached into the box and tried to subtly grab as many of the white plastic encased chemical ice packs as he could. "Who knew FBI agents had such a way with quarter horses?"

"Just like old bone docs, right?"

Drew glanced up in time to catch Doc's wink.

"Just trying to do my job, Doc."

"About that."

Drew froze in the process of filling his arms with ice

packs. There was nothing in this world that meant more to him than providing medical care to the rodeo community here in the sports medicine trailer. Other than his family, that is.

Dr. Tracer continued in the tone of voice he reserved for telling lifelong rodeo folk that they could never compete again. "I have a new job for you, Drew. Well, let's call it a new assignment."

Drew straightened slowly, clutching a wad of the squishy packs to his chest. "What sort of assignment?"

"I need you to watch over one of the saddle bronc riders here for the duration of this rodeo as well as the next three, which we happen to already be contracted for."

Watch over? Drew tucked his chin. "Who?"

"One Peyton Halliday."

Drew frowned in thought. He didn't recognize the name. He used the time it took him to stack the ice packs he held within the storage cabinet to search his memory, but still came up empty. "I don't know who that is."

"No reason you should. Unless you trade in oil futures."

Now, Drew was really confused. "Haven't gotten around to it yet. But sure, I can keep an eye on this Holiday person."

"Halliday," Doc corrected with an amused smirk that further creased his sun-weathered face. "Peyton Halliday."

"Halliday. Sorry. I'll have this Peyton Halliday drop by here once a day, and I'll check him over. Make sure he's good to go." Simple enough.

"No. That won't cut it." Doc turned away from the now empty box and went to the small computer desk at the front of the trailer and took a seat on the backless wheeled stool.

"What do you mean?"

"When I say watch over, I mean *watch over*. As in *follow around*. Hold hands, if it'll help. I need you to keep Peyton very safe. Basically, provide immediate medical care if needed. But the impression I got was they'd prefer if none is needed. The Hallidays are a very, very wealthy, philanthropic Texas oil family with an apparently newfound soft spot for rodeo folk."

Before Drew could say *so what*, having come from a very, very wealthy, philanthropic family himself, Doc continued.

"The Hallidays have offered a substantial chunk of change, which we need"—Doc waved an expansive hand at the outdated but nonetheless pristine white and chrome interior of the trailer—"in exchange."

Everything in the clinic was more than adequate, but the rodeo community they served deserved more than adequate.

"They are offering enough to update the whole shebang and keep it going for a hot minute independent of the rodeo contracts."

"A substantial chunk?" Drew asked, knowing only deep pockets could pay for the state-of-the-art equipment and fixtures Doc had been talking about needing for the trailer.

"Very substantial. Enough for the entire Sports Medicine program. The clinic. And the endless supplies we get." He gestured toward the now empty box. "And our salaries," he emphasized the last. "A chunk we will lose if you don't keep Peyton Halliday safe and sound."

"A bronc rider," Drew said flatly, mystified by how they

expected him to keep someone competing in the second most dangerous event in rodeo, eclipsed only by bull riding, safe and sound.

Doc shrugged in a *what can you do* way.

"You said they have a newfound soft spot for rodeo people," Drew said. "So, they aren't themselves rodeo people?"

"From what I gather, they own what I'd characterize as a hobby ranch where the family mostly live, but at the end of the day, they're oil people, not rodeo."

"Meaning their new rodeo philanthropy is primarily aimed at providing immediate care to their bronc rider."

"That would be my guess. But seeing as it will benefit everyone competing out in our neck of the woods, I choose not to question the Hallidays' motivation."

Doc was right. The clinic provided a very real, necessary benefit to every competitor at the rodeos held here at the High Desert Rodeo grounds and all the other rodeos in the circuit he and Doc were contracted with.

Doc continued, "We get by, for sure, but when Brian Halliday called me last week and offered us more than enough for a serious upgrade as well as additional operating capital for nothing more than keeping a close eye on a single rider with a habit of going rogue..." Doc trailed off with another shrug.

Drew nodded. And he was more than willing to do what was necessary to improve and maintain the traveling clinic he aspired to eventually take over. "Then sign me up for Peyton Halliday babysitting duty," he said.

Turning back to the desktop computer and moving the

mouse to wake the monitor, Doc said, "Already done, son."

Drew snorted and began breaking down the box the ice packs had been delivered in. He certainly didn't begrudge Doc for preemptively committing Drew to something that would protect the future of the traveling sports medicine clinic. The rodeo program had been Doc's life's work, after all. A life Drew hoped to emulate.

Folding the collapsed cardboard box into a manageable size, Drew said, "If you don't need me, I think I'll go find this precious Peyton before the start of the first round of the saddle broncs. If he's drawn one of Liam's horses, I'll see if I can finagle a trade for a less rank horse. That should go a long way toward keeping him *safe and sound*."

Doc used his cowboy booted heel to spin the stool to face Drew. "See, I knew I had the right man for the job. And don't worry about me. I'll hold down the fort. It's more important for you to stay with Halliday than be here at the clinic or hanging on the rail with me. Go, and good luck." He gave the brim of his well-worn cowboy hat a small tug in farewell then turned back to the computer.

Drew tucked the cardboard under one arm and snagged his hat off the exam table on his way out the same door he'd entered through. He deposited the cardboard in the recycle bin tucked beneath the elevated hitch of the fifth wheel and headed toward the arena.

The official rodeo wasn't set to start for at least thirty minutes, so Drew took the time to pause, pull his phone from his jeans pocket and send a text to Liam asking which of his bucking broncs he'd brought the short distance from the Wright Ranch to compete in this rodeo and which of them were the least likely to make its rider eat dirt. Drew already knew his brother would respond with something along the lines of all of his horses served up a mouthful of dirt to their riders, but Drew had to try.

Drew was just sliding his phone back into his pocket when a cheer from the stands reached him. While nowhere near as loud as the roar generated by the crowd that typically filled the stands to watch the rodeos hosted by the High Desert Rodeo grounds, the ruckus was notable for its enthusiasm. Something was clearly happening within the arena before the official start of the rodeo. Probably the introduction of the rodeo court. Or the equestrian flag team starting one of their intricate routines. Nothing like an American flag held by a pretty girl atop a well-trained horse to get the crowd cheering.

Then, as Drew wove his way past the bull and bronc pens, his eyes peeled for both his brother Liam and any cowboy wearing the tell-tale bronc rider neck padding that kept the inevitable whiplash to a minimum, the deep, booming voice of the rodeo announcer reached him over the public address system.

"All right! That's what I call a High Desert welcome to the ladies of *Buckin' TV!* Now, it's time to put your hands together for our first exhibition bronc rider. Coming to us all the way from deep in the heart of Texas, Peyton Halliday, going seat to saddle against Karen From Finance!"

Drew stopped in his tracks, trying to process what he'd just heard, but the roar of approval from the steadily growing crowd propelled him into action. He ran for the nearest arena fencing. The moment he reached it, he scrambled up onto the metal tube railing just as the bucking chute gate was pulled open. A huge paint mare erupted out into the arena with a very petite, very pretty redhead on her back. The same redhead who'd been foolish enough to accept a dare to climb on a bucking bull's back, if even for just a second.

Oh hell no.

A wave of sickening dread nearly knocked Drew off the railing. Karen From Finance was arguably Liam's rankest bucking bronc—had been for years—growing ornerier with each passing rodeo season. What had Liam been thinking allowing a horse like that to be used in a women's bronc riding exhibition?

True to form, the draft horse crossbreed had broken explosively from the chute with her head low to the ground, making it difficult for her rider to stay back in the saddle and pulling the thick, braided bronc rein taut. With one hand holding the rein and the other gripping the saddle horn as allowed in the women's circuit, the redhead, who Drew finally grasped was Peyton Halliday, looked impossibly small atop the huge horse. Yet she tenaciously maintained her seat, her long red hair flying wild beneath her cowboy hat and her chin determinedly tucked down.

After a couple of quick, teeth rattling stiff-legged hops, big Karen started to buck her rear hooves impossibly high with a twisting, lunging motion that never settled into any sort of predictable rhythm. The horse sent the loose, loamy soil and strings of spit flying with each grunting, heaving kick.

Certain he was watching an unfolding disaster, Drew gripped the top rail of the arena fence tight, anticipating the moment when Peyton Halliday would be flung to the dirt with bone-breaking violence, possibly stepped on by twelve hundred pounds of horse and in immediate need of medical aid. He prepared to launch himself over the railing and hit the ground inside the arena running.

But Peyton stayed on, something few male saddle bronc riders could do thanks to Karen's size, strength, and unpredictability.

To Drew, it felt more as if eight hours had passed, not eight seconds, before the buzzer sounded and signaled the end of the ride. Peyton Halliday had just joined a very exclusive, not to mention very male, group of bronc riders to successfully stick to Karen From Finance for the full required time.

Even though Peyton was only riding for exhibition purposes, successfully covering a horse like big Karen would significantly up her cache back on the women's saddle bronc riding circuit in Texas. Not to mention satisfying the woman in charge of the television crew following the cowgirls around the rodeo.

Drew reflexively glanced toward the catwalk above the chute Karen From Finance had rocketed from and, sure enough, immediately spotted the camera crew appearing to be raptly recording Peyton's ride. A small cluster of chaps and wide brim hat-wearing women—her fellow bronc riders, including the tall blonde—stood near, clapping and whooping. With the uneasy thought that keeping Peyton from harm might not be a simple thing with that bunch egging her on, not to mention Doc's *going rogue* comment, Drew returned his attention to the horse and woman being pursued by the pickup riders.

Not caring that the buzzer had sounded, only that a rider remained on her back, Karen kept bucking, so Drew couldn't relax his grip on the metal tube fencing until both pickup riders had pinned Karen between their mounts so one of them could pluck the petite Peyton from her saddle and veer away from the threat of the slowly settling bronc's hooves.

And it wasn't until the pickup rider helped Peyton slide safely to the dirt and she took several steps, waving her hat and grinning broadly at the cheering crowd, that Drew was able to fill his lungs with a calming breath.

He and Doc Tracer had treated more bronc riders than he could count who had suffered serious injuries without ever losing their seat. But judging from the victorious glow on her pretty face as she trotted back toward the chutes, shaking her beautiful, long red hair back so she could return her light brown cowboy hat to her head, Peyton had escaped injury.

This time.

Drew's grip tightened on the fence rail again. There was no way he could guarantee her safety during her stay in Pineville if she continued to do foolish things like climbing aboard broncs like Karen From Finance. Or any bronc, for that matter.

Drew jumped to the ground and began making his way toward the back of the chutes. There was no time like the present to tell Peyton Halliday her exhibition riding, at least at the High Desert Rodeo and the rest of his and Doc's circuit, was over.

PEYTON FELT AS if she were walking on air, not trudging through the ankle-deep soft loam of a rodeo arena, her heavy chaps slapping against her shins, after successfully covering the horse she'd traded one of her less adventurous fellow riders for. She'd just ridden the infamous Karen From Finance!

Euphoria bubbled up within her until she virtually float-ed over to the arena fencing near the base of the metal stairs that would take her back up to the catwalk where the other girls were prepping for their own rides. While she hadn't been riding with them long and they were all competitors, they counted on each other to help make sure their mounts were saddled properly and to get them on the broncs safely until they could nod for the gate to be pulled open.

And they celebrated with each other. She couldn't wait to share this incredible moment with them.

Once over the arena railing, having ignored the solicitous offers of help from nearby cowboys who'd paused in their preparations for the upcoming events to watch the spectacle of women saddle bronc riders, Peyton stripped off her leather gloves and tucked them in her back jeans pocket and headed for the stairs.

She was a step away from the base of the stairs, close enough to reach for the handrail, when a tall, broad-shouldered cowboy stepped in her path. Pulling up short, she opened her mouth to excuse herself, intending to push past him as politely as she could, when her gaze finally landed on his face. The very handsome face that she'd thought about way more than she should have ever since he'd pretty much chewed her out for accepting Sammie's dare to climb on a bull's back.

Earlier, when she'd been balanced over the big red bull's back and he'd stood in the arena on the other side of the bucking chute gate, she hadn't realized he was so tall. Granted, pretty much everyone seemed tall to her. One of the few tangible effects of the part of her childhood she thought of as the dark days.

But the heat she had noticed before behind his ice-blue eyes had intensified, and the line of his full mouth was definitely hard.

"Well, hello," she said when he continued to simply stare down at her, blocking her way.

"Peyton Halliday?" His voice was deeper than she remembered.

"Yes. Though we weren't formally introduced, were we?" She stuck out her hand and gave him her best smile. "You are?"

He looked down at her offered hand long enough that she was about to tuck it behind her, certain he was refusing it. But then he exhaled noisily through his nose and captured her hand in his, completely engulfing her much, much smaller hand within his big, warm one.

"Drew Neisson." He gave her hand one firm, yet gentle, shake before releasing it.

"Nice to meet you, Drew Neisson."

He didn't look as if he considered formally meeting her a pleasure. "I need to talk to you," he stated ominously.

She held up her hands. "Hey, I didn't hurt your family's bull. No harm, no foul, right? And in case you missed it"— she pointed toward the arena she'd just left—"I just proved I can stick to the rankest of the rank broncs—"

"That happens to belong to my family, also. The fact that you would even consider trying to ride Karen From Finance explains a lot."

She stilled. The judgment in his tone sounded an alarm in her head. "Explains a lot about what?"

He planted his hands on his lean, jeans-clad hips, further blocking her access to the stairs to the catwalk. "It explains why I have been assigned the task of keeping you safe. Which means no more bronc riding, especially on horses like Karen From Finance. Or anything else risky, for that matter."

She didn't have to ask who was behind this so-called assignment of his. The simmering frustration she'd lived with for so long, the constant itch just below her skin that she could only escape when doing something heart pumping, and yes, risky, flamed hot and prickly. But she'd had years of practice hiding her anger because letting it fly hadn't helped. At all.

And refusing to be told what she could or couldn't do ever again, Peyton simply laughed in his handsome face, pushed her way past him like she had her brothers a million times, and started up the metal stairs to the bucking chute catwalk to help her fellow riders.

CHAPTER THREE

WATCHING PEYTON HALLIDAY noisily stomp her way up the stairs to the chute catwalk with a whole lot of attitude packed into a curvy little package, Drew realized his mistake three stomps too late.

Growing up with his sister Caitlin and her best friend Amanda should have taught him to never tell a woman what she could or couldn't do. His brother Liam, who must be around here somewhere wrangling Karen From Finance, had learned that lesson the hard way while working to help Amanda save Sky High Ranch, the property that bordered the Wright Ranch. If a hot head like Liam could learn the lesson to the point Amanda had agreed to marry him, then Drew should be able to figure out a way to gain Peyton Halliday's cooperation.

But had he just blown his best chance? If he had, how would he ever tell Doc that Drew had just tanked his mentor's life's work?

Dread bubbled up in the back of Drew's throat. Trying to wipe away the feeling so he could think, he ran both hands down his face.

The booming voice of the announcer introducing the

next woman rider in the exhibition propelled Drew up the stairs to the catwalk. While he assumed that the women were riding in an exhibition to showcase what the ladies could do aboard broncs rather than a competition requiring multiple go arounds, he couldn't be sure Peyton wouldn't ride again tonight. Especially when they were being filmed for the reality TV show. He'd apologize for his initial heavy handedness and simply ask her to help him out by not riding again. Or going rogue, as Doc had said she had a tendency to do. Whatever that meant.

Intent on the bucking chute the women and their camera crew were clustered above, Drew wove his way through the cowboys and stock contractors who had collected on the catwalk to get an up-close view of the pretty cowgirls risking life and shapely limb to prove they could. Before he reached them, he'd received more than a couple of offers of assistance if any of the ladies were in need of a physical exam. Clearly, Peyton Halliday's successful ride on Karen From Finance had impressed the guys enough to open the door for such ribbing. Or they were just being cowboys. Either way, Drew simply waved them off and worked his way close enough to catch Miss Halliday's eye.

Her fierce scowl and short, sharp shake of her head let him know just how big his initial mistake had been. And when she then proceeded to completely ignore him, her attention firmly on the brunette climbing down onto a big chestnut bronc, he knew she wasn't about to talk to him again. At least not during their exhibition tonight. He had no choice but to cool his heels and hope she wouldn't ride again that night.

And if she did ride and was hurt? While he didn't doubt his and Doc's ability to put her back together again if necessary, he probably should try to come up with alternative sources of the cash they'd undoubtedly lose if Peyton ended up injured. There had to be another way to secure the funding needed for the mobile sports medicine clinic.

His attention was yanked back to the action when the gate to the bucking chute was pulled open, and the chestnut exploded into the arena. The cowboys around him automatically parted to give him clear access to the railing which he bent forward to grip, ready to leap into the arena if needed.

The brunette was too far forward and predictably lost her seat after only two bucks from the reddish-brown bronc. Fortunately, she'd obviously known she'd be bucked off and launched herself from the saddle, landing on her hands and feet like a cat. And in the next beat, she was up and running from the unpredictable flying hooves, waving a hand to signal she wasn't hurt. The wave almost instantly turned into a frustrated slap against her chaps. Male or female, no bronc rider wanted a buck-off, exhibition or no.

Drew blew out a breath and straightened, doing his best to release the tension that always gripped him until he was certain a competitor was unharmed. He loved his job, more than he'd thought possible, but he loved it best when his skills were not needed.

Knowing the sentiment was shared by Doc Tracer, Drew's gaze went to the gate where the sports medicine personnel, namely Drew and Doc, used to rush into the arena when necessary, and sure enough spotted Doc leaning against the rail. The first aid kit sat at his feet, and the backboard they employed for really bad wrecks stood propped against the fencing.

Next to him was Drew's dad and grandfather. They must have come to watch Alec compete in the marquee bull riding event later in the rodeo.

Drew took a moment to consider Douglas Neisson, wearing a chambray shirt, jeans, and black cowboy hat, and Thomas Wright, who was dressed in his usual tan suede sport coat, western-style button-down shirt, finely braided black leather bolo tie with a tasteful silver slide and matching tips. His still thick, slightly wavy silver hair was neatly combed beneath a cream cowboy hat. The most obvious alternate source of funding was his own grandfather. Thomas Wright certainly had deep enough pockets to help fund the clinic, and his long and friendly history with Doc Tracer made him the logical choice.

Drew figured the biggest hurdle he'd have to face in convincing his grandfather to step in as the funding source were the optics of one of the most prominent rough stock contractors paying for the upgrade to the medical services for the cowboys injured, sometimes severely, by the animals he provided the rodeo with. To Drew, the dual roles made sense.

Especially after what had happened to his mother, Thomas Wright's only child.

The dread, better known as stomach acid, retreated to where it belonged, and after one last quick glance at Peyton still helping her fellow lady bronc riders, Drew headed off the catwalk for where the elder members of his family were standing with his boss.

Spotting Drew, his dad broke off from whatever he'd been saying to Doc and extended an arm toward Drew in welcome. Without hesitation, Drew went to his dad and accepted the one-armed hug that ended with a hearty slap on the back.

His dad met his gaze. "Everyone good?"

As the family's lone medical professional, it was the question he was constantly asked. He didn't mind. Caring for, and about, the people around him was his thing.

Drew nodded. "Everyone's fine."

Next to Douglas, Thomas Wright pulled in a breath that expanded his barrel chest then released it slowly through his nose. People outside of the family believed the only thing the patriarch of the Wright Ranch cared about was the success of their brand, but Drew knew his grandfather would trade it all in a heartbeat if he could ensure the health and happiness of his family. The eventual loss of Drew's mother beneath the hooves of his grandfather's most prized bull had nearly broken him.

Drew's dad had broken, and some would argue he would never again be whole. Drew believed his dad had instead simply found a new way of being, one that didn't include his wife.

Drew personally never wanted to know what that would feel like.

His grandfather said, "Doc Tracer was just telling us you

weren't down here with him because you have a new assignment."

"Yes, sir." Drew stepped away from his father, not surprised his grandfather had immediately zeroed in on what was different in their world. The man had a gift. Nor was Drew surprised at his own nervousness. Thomas Wright had always been, and would always be, an intimidating man. While Drew had never, not even for one second, doubted his grandfather's love, everyone under his roof had been raised in the cowboy way. They were all expected to live each day with courage, take pride in their work, finish what they started, and do what had to be done. And Drew knew he was about to violate at least a couple of his grandfather's codes by coming to him for help.

But preserving, and if possible, improving the sports medicine clinic was worth it to Drew.

Glancing at Doc, who seemed to be watching a little too intensely the next female bronc rider trying to get the seat she wanted before she nodded, Drew said, "Can I talk to you for a minute?"

"Isn't that what we're doing?"

Drew studiously refused to fidget. "Yes sir, but—"

"Walk with me." His grandfather turned and moved farther down the arena railing.

Drew followed, and when they'd taken several steps away from Doc and Drew's dad, Drew said, "I need your help."

His grandfather's gray brows twitched upward. "With?"

"Funding for the sports medicine clinic."

"I thought you were fully funded by the rodeos Doc is

contracted with."

"We are. Barely. And the trailer could really use an up-grade." Drew hesitated but decided he needed to come clean. "My new assignment is keeping a particular bronc rider hale and hearty, exclusively, in exchange for a sizable donation for the clinic."

His grandfather shrugged. "Why would that be a prob-lem for you?"

Drew wasn't surprised by his grandfather's question be-cause Drew's reason for going into medicine had never been a secret from his family. He pulled his hat from his head and ran a hand through his hair. "Because this particular bronc rider doesn't want my ... services." Short of kidnapping her, he seriously doubted he'd be able to keep her off the broncs. But if he could have stayed close, acting as her personal physician, he could have provided her with immediate care if she needed it. Only he couldn't stay close if she didn't allow him to.

"Who is he?"

"She."

His grandfather leaned toward Drew. "Excuse me?"

"The bronc rider I'm supposed to babysit is a she."

Shifting his attention to the arena and the blonde named Sammie currently trying to maintain a hopeless seat, his grandfather asked, "One of these women bronc riders?"

Sammie finally came off the bronc and landed hard on her back, her chaps flopping upward. The crowd groaned sympathetically.

Drew watched her closely until she popped up with a

wave and ran back toward the chutes before he answered his grandfather. "Yes."

"Which one?"

Drew scanned the platform above the bucking chutes until he found Peyton. He pointed at her. "The petite redhead."

"The one who rode old Karen?"

"The very one."

His grandfather nodded thoughtfully.

Drew said, "They're doing exhibition rides at a few of the rodeos in our circuit because there is a television show filming them—"

"*Buckin' TV*."

Again, Drew wasn't surprised because his grandfather was aware of anything and everything happening in the rodeo world, regardless of the location. Drew moved to lean an elbow on the arena fence, absently watching the pickup riders herd Sammie's victorious mount toward the exit. "Right. They are filming these women while they travel around to various rodeos, proving women can ride broncs just as well as men—"

"What's her name, Drew?"

Drew pinched his nose, remembering the stubborn set of her delicate jaw while trying to forget the saucy sway of her very well-formed backside. "Peyton Halliday."

His grandfather settled back on his heels. "Presumably of the sizable-donation-to-the-clinic Hallidays."

Drew dropped his hand to the metal tube rail. "Presumably."

His grandfather crossed his arms over his still impressive chest. "And the problem is?"

The acid in Drew's stomach churned to life again. "*She* is the problem."

"This Peyton Halliday." His grandfather had a way of asking questions in the form of a statement.

"Yes. The first time I saw her earlier today she was in the process of climbing on the back of one of our bulls that Alec had sent into the chute for a practice ride on."

"Which bull was Alec—"

"It doesn't matter which bull." Drew's frustration had him interrupting his grandfather for the first time in his life. The upward twitch of one silver-gray brow had Drew quickly amending, "Red Rum. It was Red Rum."

His grandfather nodded, seemingly impressed. "But you stopped her."

"Of course, I stopped her. But later, after Doc told me he needed me to babysit her—"

"Which you agreed to?"

"Of course, I agreed. But at the time I thought Peyton Halliday was one of the male bronc riders—"

"So, Peyton being a girl is the problem?"

"No!" *Yes!* "No," he repeated with as much conviction as his unconvinced self could muster. "The problem is she refused my help." If telling her that she had to completely stop what she was doing could be described as an offer of help.

Drew found himself the recipient of the famous Thomas Wright narrowed blue-eyed laser stare. "Your help?"

Drew pushed away from the fencing at being called out for his ham-fisted approach. "Okay, I told her I'd been assigned to keep her safe and that she couldn't do anything risky—or really anything, for that matter—while she was in Pineville."

"You actually told her that."

"Of course." He'd started to sound like a broken record. "Right after she nearly gave me a heart attack by riding Karen From Finance."

"Which she did successfully."

"Yes." Which was actually pretty impressive. His grandfather clearly looked impressed. Drew waved the accomplishment off. "But she never should have been allowed on that horse in the first place. You can see what a tiny little thing she is." Drew gestured toward the chutes. "And what was Liam thinking allowing—"

"You said you'd agreed to keep her from harm while she is here?"

"I did, but—"

"Then no, I will not replace the offer of a donation if it's pulled." His grandfather uncrossed his arms and settled a heavy hand on Drew's shoulder. "You agreed to this commitment, Drew. You need to fulfill it. I know you know this."

The tinge of disappointment in his grandfather's tone made Drew's mouth dry.

His grandfather gave his shoulder a squeeze before releasing it. "I can think of worse ways to spend a week than on the tail, so to speak"—he actually winked at Drew—"of a pretty, apparently feisty cowgirl."

Drew glanced back toward the catwalk. She was pretty. Very. But she was also feisty in the bite your hand, kick you in the head kind of way. He didn't need that, now or ever.

His grandfather crossed his arms over his chest again. "Have you considered why the Hallidays want someone like you to keep an eye on her?"

"Because she's a nitwit?"

The corner of his grandfather's mouth twitched upward, but he didn't allow the smile. "Perhaps there are other reasons."

Drew looked back toward where Doc was now talking to Drew's dad, thinking about what Doc had said about the Hallidays being a very, very wealthy—as in billions?— philanthropic Texas oil family. He absently tapped his hat against his thigh. Was she in some sort of danger?

Drew rejected the notion. Her family wouldn't let her go off to travel around the country, expecting random guys like him to keep her safe. They would hire professional security providers.

Rejected or not, the notion stirred Drew's protective nature in very unexpected ways. But after everything his family had been through in the past because of a murderous former ranch hand and a local rustling ring, Drew knew a thing or two about being threatened by outside forces.

"So, you'll do it?" This time his grandfather actually asked the question rather than stating it as fact.

Drew returned his gaze to his grandfather, who was watching him intently. He fought the urge to squirm. He wasn't used to the focused attention. Now he knew why his siblings often left his grandfather's office looking so rattled.

Without his grandfather's financial help, Drew realized he had no choice if he wanted to assure that the sports medicine clinic could keep operating. Which he did. More than anything.

He tried to release some of his tension with a heavy exhale. "Yes, I'll do it," he said, resigning himself to act the glorified babysitter to an uber-rich, reckless cowgirl.

PEYTON MIGHT BE good at keeping her anger from showing, but she stunk at squashing it. For the rest of the women's first round of exhibition bronc riding, while helping make sure her fellow cowgirls' cinches were tight and that they made it into the saddle safely and for long enough that they were able to nod for the gate pull, she simmered with an ever-growing fury.

How dare her family try to control her way up here in Oregon.

She'd signed up with the *Buckin' TV* production, despite knowing full well why they'd wanted her—*little rich girl survives awful childhood illness and grows up to risk it all by becoming a ranch saddle bronc rider!*—precisely because they would take her far from her smothering family in Texas. There were no women's bronc riding circuits besides the one in Texas, so the TV show wanting to hit the road for exhibition rides outside of Texas had been what she'd thought the perfect solution for her.

She should have known distance wouldn't dampen her family's need to restrict what she tried to do with her life. And what she wanted to do with her life was experience everything this amazing world had to offer. If it got the human heart pumping, she wanted to do it.

At least once.

Which was how she'd become a saddle bronc rider. Spending most of her post-hospital years on her family's hobby ranch had instilled in her a deep love of all things horse. But the day she'd snuck a ride on a green-broke horse and had managed to stick in the saddle despite the young animal's best efforts to put her in the dirt, she'd found a new level of adrenaline rush.

But now her family was doing their best to take this away from her, too.

Normally, she'd simply ignore their efforts and keep doing what she was doing, but she didn't think she'd be able to shake her anger until she'd let them know exactly how she felt about this latest intrusion into her life. She was twenty-five years old, after all. A grown woman. It was time they let her live her own life.

So, as soon as the night's exhibition ride was over and despite Nat's insistence all the girls hang on the rails for the camera and watch the men ride—because no matter how bad-ass the woman, apparently, she still just wanted a cowboy—Peyton snagged her saddle and slipped away to make her first and only call home.

She returned to the small trailer she had to herself, the

one parental insistence she'd acquiesced to, because if she were to get hurt or, God forbid, sick again, she didn't want anyone seeing it. The matching silver pickup truck she absolutely adored was unfortunately spending its week in little Pineville at Bud's Repair Shop getting a new transmission. Fortunately, the gears hadn't started to slip until they were almost to the High Desert Rodeo grounds, so she'd been able to park her trailer in the competitors' mobile village before taking the truck in for repair.

Once inside the trailer, she placed her saddle on its frame and locked the door behind her. She didn't take the time to remove her boots or chaps, instead simply dropping her hat on the little table and grabbing up her phone.

Peyton stared at her contact list for a moment, trying to decide who to call. She settled on the family member most likely to bring in reinforcements in the form of a bossy cowboy. Sliding into the dining booth seat, she touched her finger to the screen and put the phone to her ear and waited to connect.

"Peyton?" Brian Halliday answered on the first ring. Heir to Texas oil tycoon Harold Halliday's billions, her dad never had his phone out of reach.

But he was a busy man, so she started at his quick answer. "Yes, it's me. Hi."

"Are you okay? Were you hurt?"

Peyton winced at the fear in his voice. "I'm fine, Dad. Really. I'm good." She truly hated worrying her family. She loved them. Dearly. But she needed them to understand that she had to live her life the way she needed to.

"Thank God." She heard his exhale of relief clearly through the phone. "Do you need something? Money? I can deposit more money into your account right now."

Peyton rubbed her forehead. She hated this so much. He really did just want to take care of her. But she wasn't that sick little girl with the leaky heart anymore.

"No, Dad. I don't need money."

"Okay…" He sounded skeptical. In his world, everyone needed money.

Her anger left her in a rush. "I just want you to know that I don't need anyone babysitting me or stopping me from doing what I was hired to do."

"Peyton—"

"Please, Dad. Just listen to me. I'm not a child. I know what I can and can't do, and I'll never try to do anything that I'm not certain I can safely handle. You have to believe me."

He sighed heavily again. "I do believe you, Peyton. I know full well how strong and talented you are."

"Then why did you arrange for someone here to stop me? It was you, wasn't it?"

"It was." He suddenly sounded older than his sixty years. "But I did it because it was the only way I could stop your brothers from coming after you and hauling you back home. They saw the first episode of that show you are involved in, and they were not happy about it."

Leaning forward, Peyton dropped her suddenly hot forehead against the cool Formica tabletop. She was so screwed.

"I convinced them I had it handled by arranging for Dr.

Andrew Neisson to keep an eye on you. Tell me I have it handled, Peyton."

She let out her own heavy breath. "You have it handled, Dad. I love you."

"I love you, too, Peyton honey. Be safe. And have fun."

He ended the call, and all Peyton could think was it looked as though she was now officially stuck with the cowboy doctor.

CHAPTER FOUR

D REW MAY HAVE resigned himself to his role as glorified babysitter to an uber-rich reckless cowgirl, but he was a long, long way from being happy about it.

Apparently, Sammie had been the last of the women bronc riders, concluding the exhibition rides right before the start of the night's official rodeo.

After speaking with his grandfather who'd then left with Drew's dad to find Alec, Drew watched the women leave the platform above the bucking chutes. They'd undoubtedly gone to reclaim their saddles from their respective broncs' stock contractors. He lost sight of a certain redhead, but he assumed she couldn't be hurt—or find some way to *go rogue*—simply lugging a saddle. So, he returned to his usual spot next to Doc to watch the start of the regular rodeo.

"Did you find Peyton?" Doc asked when he reached him.

Drew took the time to thread his arms through the metal fencing and hook a cowboy boot heel on the lowest rung so he could lean on the fence. "I did."

"And?" Doc ran a critical eye over him. The man had a lot in common with Drew's grandfather. Neither one missed a thing.

"And I now understand why her family wants someone keeping a close eye her."

Doc grunted.

Drew's gaze flicked to where the women bronc riders and their camera crew were setting down their retrieved saddles and making a spot for themselves at the arena railing next to the bucking chutes. Still no Peyton. Maybe she was using the restroom or something.

As the mounted drill team performed their rodeo-opening routine, he and Doc fell silent out of habit and watched carefully. While they might not be competing in an event, the drill team members were nonetheless mounted on spirited, half-ton animals that were known to occasionally take exception to flags being waved past their heads with bone-breaking results. Thankfully tonight the drill team finished and charged from the arena without incident.

"A real pistol, eh?" Doc picked up their conversation as if they hadn't stopped talking.

"Something like that."

"Which one is she?" Doc tipped the brim of his cowboy hat toward the conspicuous line of Buckin' Babes now seated atop the fence.

"She isn't with the rest of them right now."

Doc shot him a sharp look. "Where is she?"

"I don't know." He almost told Doc that the last time he had seen Peyton Halliday was when she'd laughed in his face and pushed her way past him after he'd failed miserably at telling her he'd been assigned to keep her safe. But disappointing Doc was about as appealing as letting his grandfather down.

"Then why are you standing here?"

Drew pointed at the med kit on the ground at their feet and gestured toward the arena as the first male bronc rider and his mount burst from a chute. The cowboy, a local kid who had gone to school with Alec, stayed aboard the sorrel bronc for a total of three hopping bucks before he sailed off. Both Drew and Doc stilled. The cowboy hit the dirt hard but popped up and scrambled away from the threat of flying hooves. They tracked his movements, watching for any hitch in his gate or droop of the shoulders, but he looked fine.

Drew opened his mouth with the intention of saying he was doing his job, but Doc's slow head shake stopped him.

"I told you, your job—your only job—while Miss Halliday is visiting our circuit is to shadow her like the evening sun. I can handle this." Doc flicked a hand at the next bronc rider currently trying to stay on one of Liam's broncs while scoring as many points as possible. "Been doing it since before you were born."

Which was precisely why Drew wanted to help Doc. He knew better than to argue though.

Doc continued, "Go. Find her. Make sure she isn't up to something."

As Drew turned away to do as he'd been told, he grumbled, "Yeah, 'cause that's a great use of a medical degree."

"Think of it as bedside manner training," Doc called after him, then snorted a laugh.

Drew acknowledged Doc's idea of humor with a wave of his hand and a "Yes, sir" as he walked away toward the women bronc riders perched on the arena railing being filmed hooting and hollering at the male riders. Drew wanted nothing more than to turn on his heel and walk away. But not too far because there was still a rodeo going on. And where there was a rodeo, there would undoubtedly be injured competitors. His conscience wouldn't allow him to not render aid.

He had to weave his way through the knot of cowboys clustered behind the ladies, cowboys clearly more interested in the view of the ladies' backsides than in the chance of getting on television. They definitely weren't watching the rodeo.

Drew recognized one of the cowboys. "Hey, Danny. Don't you have some of Bodie's bulls to tend to?"

Danny Kline, one of Drew's brother-in-law's ranch hands, glanced at him. "Drew." He lifted his chin in greeting. "Cabe is with our bulls. The view is way better here. What are you doing on this side of the arena?"

The locals were used to seeing Drew and Doc Tracer near their medical gear and the gate they always used.

Not sure if he should reveal the specifics of his assignment, Drew said, "I'm keeping an eye on…" He gestured to the women atop the fence.

Danny snorted. "Ain't we all, brother. Ain't we all."

Drew touched a finger to his hat and continued to press his way through the crowd. He finally made it to where Sammie was seated, her long, chaps-encased legs swinging inside the arena.

"Sammie," Drew called up to her.

All of the women turned to look down on him.

Her pretty face erupted in a wide smile. "Hey, it's bull boy!"

He heaved a sigh. While he didn't regret intervening to stop their high jinks with Red Rum, maybe he could have handled it differently. "Do you know where Peyton is?"

She twisted on the top rail to face him more. "She didn't hurt your family's bull. We were just playing around—"

Drew held up a hand. "No, that's not why…" He sighed again and planted his hands on his hips. "I just need to find her."

Her smile turned speculative, just as it had when he and Alec had told her and Peyton they were part of the Wright Ranch family. "She's in her trailer."

Fully aware there was a virtual sea of competitors' trailers behind him, he pushed for specifics. "Which is where, exactly?"

She raised a hand to point, but the brunette next to her nudged her with an elbow and shook her head.

Finally, someone with sense. Revealing the location of one of Buckin' Babes's trailers in front of a bunch of fanboy cowboys wouldn't have been the smartest thing to do. Unfortunately, smart discretion wasn't what Drew needed at the moment.

"Will she be back?" He glanced at the camera crew in time to see the woman he'd assumed to be the producer staring right at him and tugging on the cameraman's arm. Drew shifted so the cowboy next to him provided a screen for him. He seriously doubted her family, not to mention his, wanted any of this to become a part of the Buckin' Babes show.

The brunette said, "But there's the meet and greet at two, tomorrow."

Sammie's smile widened. "That's right. All of us will be available for selfies and autographs tomorrow."

"At two," he repeated.

Her smile turned sugary sweet. "At two."

Drew pressed his lips together but actually was relieved by the women protecting each other. "Right. Okay. Thanks."

While he had no intention of waiting until two o'clock tomorrow afternoon to talk to Peyton again, let alone waiting in line, he knew that short of knocking on every single competitor's trailer, he wasn't going to be able to start his new *assignment* tonight. Unless she returned to join her fellow riders, which was why he had no choice but to remain here as part of the ogling crowd of cowboys.

And if she didn't return? Drew could only hope Peyton Halliday didn't do anything stupid until tomorrow.

THE BANG OF knuckles knocking on the closed metal door of the trailer brought Peyton's attention up from the bronc rein rope she'd been rebraiding. After speaking with her father and agreeing to allow Andrew Neisson to shadow her to forestall any of her brothers from showing up, which would probably end with her locked inside her trailer while they hauled it back home to Texas, she hadn't felt like returning to the arena for Nat's *candid footage* with the rest of the girls.

Peyton preferred to hold her pity party in the privacy of her little trailer, with no one the wiser. Besides, she'd grown to love being alone in her cozy little haven, with no one asking how she was or what she intended to do next. She was free to simply be.

Afraid it was Nat coming to haul her out to join the other girls or, worse, a particular Neisson coming to try and start his babysitting gig, Peyton remained still and quiet.

The door rattled again beneath another pounding knock. Then the door handle jiggled as whoever it was tried to open the locked door.

Peyton dropped the soft braided rein to her lap. Who—?

"Peyton? Open up. It's Sammie."

Peyton blew out a relieved breath. "Just a second, Sammie." She set the rein aside on the bench and rose to go unlock the trailer door.

The second she'd freed the latch, the door jerked outward, and Sammie stepped up into the trailer. She was still wearing her fringed chaps and dirt-streaked baby-blue shirt she'd ridden in. But being Sammie, her long blonde curls were still perfectly formed and bouncy beneath her cowboy hat, and her lip gloss looked fresh.

"Did he come here? Were you locking him out?" Sammie asked in a rush, her gaze searching the interior of the little trailer.

Though she figured she already knew, Peyton asked, "Who?"

"Bull boy."

Peyton raised her brows.

"The cute cowboy who told you to stop messing with his family's bull. He's looking for you. Earlier, he was at the arena asking where you are."

Peyton went back to the bench and sat down, pulling the bronc rope back into her lap and picking up the unraveled end she'd been working on. "What did you guys tell him?"

Sammie removed her wide-brimmed felt hat from her head and deposited it next to Peyton's on the table. "The truth. That you had gone back to your trailer. Because dang, Peyton, he is *fine*." She made a show of fanning herself.

Dread swelled in Peyton's belly, and her gaze automatically jumped to the small window over the little table. The cheery blue and white checked curtains were still pulled open to allow in the warm glow of the portable lights set up around the temporary village of trailers and RVs the competitors lived in while traveling the rodeo circuit. Neisson was undoubtedly tall enough that she'd be able to see him approach, just as he'd be able to see into the trailer. She quickly reached to yank the curtains closed.

Sammie went to the small refrigerator and opened it. "Don't freak out. I didn't tell him which trailer is yours." She pulled a green bottle of sparkling water from the fridge and twisted it open with a hiss of carbonation then slid onto the table bench.

Peyton nearly deflated with relief. She retrieved the rope from her lap that she'd unwittingly dropped.

"But…" Sammie trailed off with a poorly suppressed

smile.

Peyton froze.

"Laura did tell him about the meet and greet tomorrow at two, and I mentioned how we would all be at the arena then signing autographs and taking selfies with people." Sammie stretched her legs out and took a swig of water. "That way you'll be all primped and pretty when he shows up to see you. You can thank me later."

Peyton dropped her head back against the bench. "He doesn't give a rat's patootie what I look like. He's only looking for me because he has to."

Sammie instantly sobered. "Your family?"

Peyton lifted her head and met Sammie's worried gaze. While the other woman might not know everything about Peyton, they had grown close enough for Sammie to be able to put more than a few things together. Namely how overprotective her family was and how the endless smothering fueled Peyton's need to bust loose.

"Yes. Apparently, they—or more specifically, my father—has arranged for him—Dr. Andrew Neisson—to keep an eye on me while I'm here in Pineville."

"He's a doctor?"

Peyton nodded. "With the sports medicine clinic."

Sammie snorted. "I can think of worse fates than having a guy like that keeping an eye, or all sorts of other things, on me."

Not sharing the sentiment, Peyton simply huffed in response.

"A doctor and a member of the Wright Ranch family."

Sammie sighed wistfully, then reached into her pocket for her phone.

Peyton watched Sammie type something into her smartphone, then spend a moment reading. "What are you doing?"

"Googling your babysitter, of course. There's not much on him, besides where he went to school, and that kind of boring stuff, but it says he has three brothers and a sister, and—"

Dreading the thought of what anyone could find out about her and her family from the internet, Peyton cut Sammie off. "No offense, but I don't care. Really. All I care about is how annoying he's going to be."

Sammie tucked her phone away and sat up. "Well, there's one way to keep him from being annoying."

"How?"

"Just wrap him around your little finger. He'll let you do whatever you want then."

Peyton groaned, remembering how formidable he'd looked when he'd blocked her path to the catwalk.

Undeterred, Sammie said, "So what are you going to wear for tomorrow? How are you going to do that amazing hair of yours? Curly or straight?"

Peyton released another noisy breath. "I'll probably wear these jeans. And I'll wear my hair however it dries after I wash it. Which will probably be curly."

Sammie rolled her eyes at Peyton's lack of concern for her appearance. Then she grinned. "I have an idea. Let's see if Nat will pay for us to go shopping tomorrow morning. We can get you some new jeans for the meet and greet." She eyed Peyton's well-worn and well-loved jeans as if they were molded from cow pies.

Peyton rolled her own eyes but had to admit Sammie's idea wasn't bad. Being filmed trying on clothes would be far better than having to spend another morning sitting with her fellow female bronc riders talking about how hot the local cowboys were. Peyton simply wasn't interested. The last thing she needed was another guy telling her what she shouldn't be doing.

Especially when she knew she'd have one in particular on her mind.

DREW STIFLED A yawn and scrubbed a hand over his face as he drove through town on his way to the rodeo grounds from the Wright Ranch. He hadn't slept much at all, mostly drifting from one worst-case scenario involving Peyton Halliday and bucking broncs to another. Obviously, none of them ended well. Except for the one where he stuffed her in a feed sack and locked her in the old barn. He was kind of fond of that one.

He turned his truck onto Main Street, operating mostly on muscle memory. How did her family expect him to keep her from harm when she was doing what she was doing? Riding saddle broncs and harm went hand-in-hand, for Pete's sake. If they were so concerned about her safety, why didn't they simply keep her safe at home?

He'd already driven by the cluster of women, laughing and smiling with their many shades of long hair flowing from beneath the array of colorful cowboy hats before they registered in his brain. Since groups of pretty women weren't by any means a rarity in town, the rodeo court being a case in point, it wasn't until Drew spotted the camera crew trailing behind them that he slowed his truck enough for a backward glance. Sure enough, the shortest of the group had long waves of beautiful dark red hair lifting in the breeze beneath her cream hat.

Peyton Halliday.

Just her name elicited a very unwanted endocrine response.

The Buckin' Babes were entering a women's clothing boutique that shared the same type of old west facade and linking covered boardwalk as every other building on Main Street. Drew had never in his entire life been inside the boutique, despite it being on the main drag in town and located directly across from the diner everyone in the area, including him, frequented. While he doubted the shop contained anything that could cause even the most reckless of cowgirls harm, after the sleepless night he'd just had, he didn't want to make a mistake by not keeping eyes on her as much as he could.

And because of the sleepless night he'd just had, Drew pulled his truck into a street parking spot in front of the specialty coffee shop at the end of Main Street, bought himself a coffee, and then hustled down the boardwalk. The hard heels of his cowboy boots were loud against the rough-hewn planks. No way would he risk the chance to improve the clinic by not being able to say he kept tabs on her no matter what she was doing, and there was no better time to start than now.

He took up a position in front of the boutique with his shoulder propped against one of the rough-hewn posts supporting the boardwalk's cover to drink his coffee. Even from outside, he could hear the women. They were clearly enjoying themselves.

The boutique's door opened, and Sammie emerged, her attention firmly on Drew. Her smile widened. "Bull Boy! I thought that was you. Why are you lurking around out here all by your lonesome?"

Before he could respond in any way, she hurried toward him and grabbed his arm, pulling him away from the post toward the door. "Come on! Join us."

While it was the last thing he wanted to do, he allowed her to pull him along as she yanked open the boutique's door. Once inside, Sammie turned as if to speak to him, but her name being called stopped her. The brunette who had told him about the meet and greet was beckoning her. Sammie gave his arm a pat and released him so she could rejoin the women, and Drew came to a grinding halt.

It took him a moment to process what he was seeing. The tiny women's western wear shop was teaming with people, the three-member camera crew—dressed all in black, for some reason—stood out to him first. They were already filming the group of happily chattering women bronc riders. Then he spotted Peyton within the group, and he had to fight the overwhelming urge to back himself right out of the boutique.

Peyton, sans cowboy hat and boots, was modeling a new pair of very sparkly, very snug jeans and what he thought at first glance to be a red and white bandanna but turned out to be a halter top. Drew's mouth went dry despite the coffee he'd just sipped as he watched her toss her beautiful long red curls over her shoulder and look back at the camera, her smile outshining the crystals and rhinestones decorating the pockets of the jeans she was trying to highlight with a not-so-subtle arch of her back.

Her beauty and obvious spunk hit Drew square in the chest in a way he'd never experienced before. Sweat popped out beneath the brim of his hat, and the palm of his hand grew damp against the paper coffee cup. He had to fight the urge to back out of the shop again. But he wasn't standing here because of Peyton's obvious allure. He was here because he had to be to protect the future he'd been working toward for years now. If his reaction to her was any indication, he was in big trouble.

He'd best keep his perspective. This was a job, and he'd tackle it clinically just like he had every other aspect of his job. He would not allow any sort of personal connection with his *assignment*.

Nat, with her dark hair pulled back into a low ponytail and a black T-shirt tucked into black jeans, turned toward the door, and caught sight of him. After saying something to the cameraman who nodded in acknowledgment, she gestured for him to come forward.

Drew stayed put. He was absolutely not here to be on television.

"Hey," Nat said and came toward him when he didn't move. "You're from the rodeo, right?"

While her question would be answered in the affirmative by pretty much everyone in Pineville, he gave a short nod by way of acknowledgment and took another drink of coffee.

Nat's gaze traveled over him in a sharp, speculative way. "Do you want to be on TV?"

"Absolutely not."

She narrowed her eyes. "Then why are you in here?"

He lifted his chin toward Peyton, who was laughing, a surprisingly husky sound that tightened his stomach, as she did an exaggerated imitation of a runway walk. "I've been asked to keep an eye on her."

"By her family?" Nat didn't sound at all surprised.

Drew met her dark brown eyes. She probably knew more about the Hallidays than Drew. "Yes."

She offered him her hand. "Natalie Polk. Executive producer. Call me Nat."

Drew shook her hand. "Drew Neisson."

She pointed at his shirt. "Dr. Andrew Neisson?"

He glanced down at where she had pointed. He'd forgotten he was wearing his official sports medicine shirt with his name embroidered in red over the breast pocket of the white button-down as well as the mobile clinic's logo. "That's me."

She nodded knowingly. "Makes sense. It's a good thing you have advanced medical training. You'll need it around that one." She gestured toward Peyton.

At that exact same moment, Peyton's gaze caught on them, and her entire expression changed. The lightness fell away from her pretty face, replaced by what Drew could only think of as wariness. After saying something to Sammie who'd joined her, Peyton dipped back into one of the changing rooms.

Nat continued, "Yep, that one's a handful. But she makes for damn good television."

Drew brought his back teeth together. Not anymore, if he had anything to say about it.

CHAPTER FIVE

PEYTON ESCAPED BACK into the small dressing room, yanking the privacy curtain closed as her heart threatened to pound out of her chest.

He was here.

Mr. Too Tall Bossy Pants with the icy-hot eyes was here, and she was stuck in a dressing room. She caught sight of herself in the full-length mirror and groaned. She was wearing the most ridiculous thing ever. The jeans were cute, aside from needing about a foot cut off the hem. But the halter top...what had she been thinking?

She stripped off the outfit and grabbed for her own clothes, dressing as fast as she could.

She was just pulling her favorite Dallas Cowboys T-shirt over her head when the curtain rattled and began to open. Peyton lurched back against the mirror, struggling to get her T-shirt on.

She heard Sammie hiss, "Peyton."

Peyton got her head through the neck of the white and blue shirt and saw Sammie sticking her head into the little dressing room, the curtain tucked tightly beneath her chin and held closed against the doorframe.

"Peyton!" Sammie said more insistently.

"Geez, Sammie. What?" Though she was pretty sure she already knew.

"He's here."

Peyton used the excuse of straightening her shirt to avoid meeting Sammie's gaze. "He who?"

"Dr. Bull Boy. The guy your parents…you know."

Peyton was thankful Sammie hadn't actually said, *the guy your parents hired to babysit you.*

"I spotted him skulking around outside, and I drug him in."

Peyton paused, fastening her belt buckle. "You what? Why would you do that?"

"So you can start wrapping him around your finger. Duh." Sammie nodded toward the skimpy red top Peyton had just taken off. "Now is the perfect time."

Not at all in agreement, Peyton grabbed for her boots, keeping her gaze adverted. She didn't want Sammie to see just how rattled having him here made her. How the way he'd been looking at her as she goofed around for the other girls had launched her heart into her throat.

As nonchalantly as she could, she said, "Okay."

"Okay?" Sammie frowned, clearly skeptical. "What do you mean, okay?"

Peyton dropped one boot and looked at Sammie. "What am I supposed to say?" she whispered. "It's not like there's an escape door in this dressing room."

Sammie rolled her eyes. "That's not what I meant. What are you going to say to him?"

Peyton considered some possible responses. *Drop dead?* No, too harsh. *Step off, big fella?* That would do. If there wasn't a camera crew trained on her. But there was, so instead, she answered, "Hello?"

Sammie blinked. "Seriously?"

"If Nat has Dan filming, then definitely." Normally she didn't care if she was being filmed or not, but there was no way she'd try to *wrap him around her finger*, or the alternative, create a scene on camera that could in anyway embarrass her family. She knew she worried them and felt bad about it, but she would never deliberately embarrass them.

As soon as she and Drew were away from the crew though, she would set the ground rules. She would make it very clear that while she had no choice but to allow him to follow her around—or whatever else he intended to do—the one thing he would not do would be to keep her from experiencing everything worth experiencing while she was in Pineville.

Peyton stomped her feet into her town boots, turned to the mirror long enough to make sure her shirt was straight and pulled down all the way and that her zipper was all the way up, grabbed her hat, then turned to the curtain.

Sammie snorted out a laugh and dropped the edge of the curtain to point at Peyton. "Umm, your hair."

Peyton spun back toward the mirror to find her hair standing up in a red halo of static electricity. She tried smoothing it down but settled for mashing it beneath her hat.

Sammie shrugged. "Good enough." She threw open the

curtain with a loud rattle of the metal rings and stepped back to allow Peyton to step out.

She'd intended to ignore the very tall cowboy scowling by the door until the girls and camera crew left the boutique, but her gaze went immediately to his. And instantly found herself trapped by his icy heat. It wasn't until she caught the movement of Nat directing Dan to train his camera on her that she was able to pull herself away his thrall.

Tugging the brim of her hat low enough to block the tractor beam her babysitter probably called eyes, Peyton whispered to Sammie, "I need a distraction."

"I'd say one just walked through the door."

Peyton picked up a folded pair of jeans and pretended to admire them. "No, I don't need a distraction for myself. I need you to create a distraction for Nat so I can get you know who out of camera range until I can set some ground rules."

Sammie bent her head as if checking the price tag on a shirt. "He doesn't look like the type who likes to be told what to do. And coming from the family he does, I'm not surprised."

"Well, he must be a little okay with being told what to do, or else he wouldn't be here right now. Can you create a distraction?"

Sammie grinned broadly. "One distraction coming right up." She dropped the price tag and looked to the other bronc riders. "Ladies," she said loudly enough to gain their attention, then clapped her hands with a quick yet pointed look toward the camera crew. "Let's have a New Hat Show! Come on, everyone grab a hat off the display over there, model it, then we'll vote on the best hat and cowgirl match."

Nat lit up. "Yes, excellent idea, Sammie. Do as she suggests, ladies." Then she started positioning Dan with his camera and Phil with the boom mic.

The other girls cheered and whooped and jostled to get to the wall lined with display shelves full of cowboy hats.

Peyton used the commotion to slip toward Dr. Andrew Neisson, still standing near the boutique's door with coffee in hand and watching the spectacle from beneath the brim of his pristine white felt cowboy hat. When she made for the door, he smoothly stepped in front of her just as he had when he'd tried to stop her from going up the stairs to the bucking chutes catwalk.

She dipped around him just as smoothly, but grabbed the sleeve of his logoed, crisp white cotton button-down shirt and tugged him with her. "Outside," she said quietly as she pushed the door open.

Thankfully, he followed without a word.

She let go of his sleeve and continued walking down the boardwalk until they were well clear of the boutique's windows. But she still felt too exposed.

"Hey, Miss Halliday."

Annoyance flaring, she stopped abruptly and turned to face him just in time to see him reaching for her. He dropped his hand to his side without touching her.

She looked up at his handsome face, trying her best to ignore his perfect square jaw, straight nose, and expressive mouth. "Is there some place we can talk?"

"We are talking."

"Some place private." She glanced pointedly at a group of teens loitering in front of the boutique behind him, drawn by the lure of a reality TV show cast and crew.

He gave a quick nod. "The diner." He pointed across the street, where the businesses sported a near mirror image of western facades and wooden boardwalk. The Pineville Diner had taken the old west theme one step further with wagon wheel accents she found quaint.

"Perfect." She waited for a noisy diesel dually truck to pass then started across the two-lane street. The late-morning sun was bright and hot once out of the shade provided by the tall facades.

Drew's bootheels rapped on the pavement as he caught up with her. When he reached her side, he said, "Don't you have to be back there making a show of trying on hats with the rest of ladies?"

"We're professional ranch saddle bronc riders, not *ladies*."

When he didn't reply, she glanced up at him. He was holding his mouth firmly shut. Clearly not willing to risk sticking his foot in it. Smart man.

They stepped up onto the boardwalk, and he dropped his disposable coffee cup into a wood-clad garbage can with a wet clatter. Peyton reached for the small wagon wheel that had been halved to form pulls on each side of the diner's double door. His longer arms allowed him to grab hold of the handle first, and he pulled the door open and held it for her.

Used to her brothers' rather aggressive form of chivalry, she muttered a thanks and stepped into the diner. The difference between the bright, early summer sun and the dimness of the diner interior had her pulling up short to allow her eyes to adjust.

Big, warm hands settled on her waist and eased her forward with a gentle but firm nudge.

The contact sent her lurching into the *seat yourself* sign standing in front of the hostess pedestal.

"Whoa, easy there," he said gently, as if soothing a spooked animal.

Embarrassment heated her cheeks. Hopefully, the muted light given off by the wagon wheel chandeliers was poor enough to hide her blush.

"This way." Drew stepped around her and started to walk toward one of the booths lining both walls. The restaurant wasn't large, a little on the narrow side but deep. There was only a smattering of tables with ladderback chairs in the center of the space. Just a few of the booths were occupied by diners.

A waitress who looked to be in her late twenties turned from the kitchen pass-through and spotted them. Her pretty face lit up.

"Hey, Doctor Drew! I'm surprised to see you more than ten steps from the sports medicine rig when there's a rodeo in town." She grabbed a couple of menus and came toward the booth Drew had chosen.

Drew pulled his hat from his head. "Hi, Meg. Just here to grab a bite with a friend."

Meg eyed Peyton as she came up behind Drew, who stood waiting for Peyton to slide into the booth before he took his seat across from her. Probably every single woman in the area kept a keen eye on members of Thomas Wright's family. Peyton's brothers got the same treatment back home. They'd always reacted with amusement. Drew didn't seem to notice at all.

Setting his hat on the red leather bench next to him, Drew made the introductions. "Meg, this is Peyton Halliday. Peyton, meet Meg Burton."

After setting the menus down so she could pull her notepad and pencil from her apron, Meg smiled and gave Peyton a nod. "Nice to meet you—hey"—she aimed the eraser end of the pencil at Peyton's Cowboys T-shirt—"aren't you one of those lady bronc riders from Texas putting on that exhibition?"

"Yeah. I am." Peyton resisted the urge to squirm. One thing she knew for sure was that she wasn't doing it for the fame or notoriety. She removed her own hat, hoping her hair wasn't still standing on end, and set it next to her on the bench seat as Drew had.

"Wow. That is so cool. I'd never have the courage to do something like that. But it's probably a good thing you're friends with a sports medicine guy."

Peyton shot Drew a glance. Would he admit they weren't actually friends?

He picked up a menu and handed it to Peyton. "She happens to be a very good bronc rider. She only needs me for lunch recommendations."

Peyton nearly gaped at him. Had he just complimented her? Had he watched her ride and thought she'd done well? A strange sort of pleasure mixed with pride wound through her at the notion. She looked down at the menu. "Oh yeah? So, what do you recommend?"

He looked up at Meg. "What's the sandwich special today?"

"Reuben."

He handed her his menu. "I definitely recommend the Reuben. That's what I'll have."

"Then Reuben it is." Peyton handed over her menu, too.

"Good choice." Meg smiled. "What'll you have to drink?"

Drew looked to Peyton, so she said, "Sweet tea?"

Meg raised her brows.

Drew said, "Make that two iced teas. But bring the sweeteners."

"I'll get those right up." Meg left and went to the long, narrow window open to the kitchen.

As soon as Meg was out of earshot, Peyton said, "Do you really think I'm a good bronc rider?"

Drew fiddled with his hat on the bench next to him. "I saw you ride Karen From Finance. Yeah, you're good."

Satisfaction blossomed in her chest. "So, no more *no bronc riding, especially on horses like Karen From Finance, or anything else risky?*" She imitated his deep, stern voice as best she could.

He shook his head. "Sorry. You still can't do those things."

She flopped back against the bench. Her blood started a slow, steady boil, and she thought, *Yeah, watch me.*

It was time to do what she'd come in here to do and lay down the ground rules with Dr. Drew.

"Here's the deal. I'll let you follow me around so you can fulfill this so-called assignment of yours, but I'm going to do what I'm going to, got it?"

He simply *hmphed*, his pale blue eyes unblinking.

Clearly, she'd have to be smart about getting around Drew's nanny act or else she'd find herself fending off her brothers in person here in Pineville. She'd have to try a different tact.

Meg returned to their booth with two tall glasses of iced tea and a container of different types of sweetener packets.

"Thanks, Meg," Drew said.

Peyton took a sip, made a face at the bitter taste, then grabbed the sugar packets. As she sweetened her tea, Drew looked at her strangely, so she mused, "You do realize I'm contractually obligated to participate in the exhibition."

"I'll write a medical exemption."

Peyton stilled. Had they told him? Is that why he looked so pissed? But she wasn't quitting that easily. One thing she was very good at was not quitting.

She leaned forward, folding her hands atop the table. "Is that what you do for the cowboys who have busted every bone in their body but still climb on their next ride because they've signed a contract with a sponsor who expects them to ride?"

He leaned forward also, planting his elbows on the table.

"I offer to. Every. Damn. Time." The pale blue of his eyes darkened dramatically.

She told herself it was because of the dim lighting, but the hard set of his jaw made her think otherwise.

So much for that tact.

She heaved a sigh, then suddenly remembered something his brother had said after he'd realized who she and Sammie were. He'd accused Drew of not paying attention to anything outside of his medical books. It occurred to Peyton there was more than one way to win over a stubborn cowboy.

To find out if it was true that Drew was all work and no play, Peyton asked, "What do you do for fun, Drew?"

He absently swirled the ice in his tea. "Medical school, residency, and now a sports medicine fellowship doesn't leave much time for fun."

She nodded as if in commiseration but was actually thinking his brother had been right. Maybe if she showed him what living—really living—looked like, he'd discover as she had how much fun it could be. The idea definitely had possibilities. As long as she kept her heart out of the equation, showing Drew how to live might just be the way to manage this doctor cowboy.

And she'd be able to do what she wanted without her family being the wiser.

IF DREW THOUGHT watching Peyton Halliday model snug

sparkly jeans and a skimpy top was a threat to his composure, watching her take a sip of unsweetened iced tea and the resulting face she'd made had done the strangest things to his gut.

She was a beautiful woman, with all that glorious red hair and nearly topaz hazel eyes. And the strength she'd shown, not just of body but mostly of will, when she'd stuck to the back of Karen From Finance, was stunning. But when she'd screwed up her face after tasting the tea that was clearly far different from the sweet tea she was obviously used to drinking down in Texas, she'd become the most adorable thing he'd ever seen.

She had an impish quality that had nothing to do with her height but everything to do with her spirit. She was a ball of fun ready to be unraveled. If he wasn't careful, he'd find himself tangled up in her shenanigans.

And he feared his dealings with her—necessary for the future he'd dreamed of—were about to become the furthest thing from clinical and drift into the highly personal. As much as he didn't want to admit it, there was something about this woman that rattled his cage. Which was not something he could let happen. Not only was his future on the line, but he wasn't about to put his heart at risk.

Losing someone he loved, again, just wasn't worth it.

CHAPTER SIX

WITH A PLAN for how to deal with her tagalong cowboy firmly established in her mind, Peyton leaned back against the booth seat and prepared to devour the delicious-looking sandwich Meg had just set in front of her. The oversized sandwich was nestled next to crispy fries in a classic red basket lined with red and white checked paper. Perfect.

Drew said, "Thank you, Meg."

"Anytime, Drew." She winked at him. To Peyton, she said, "Enjoy."

"Thank you, Meg." She watched the waitress leave, but the luscious smell of thinly sliced corned beef, sauerkraut, melty swiss cheese, and drippy Thousand Island between toasted light and dark rye swirled bread made her mouth water and claimed her attention. She glanced up at Drew and found him watching her. She told herself the hungry look on his face was inspired by the sandwich sitting on the table in front of him.

"Just wait until you taste it."

She grinned. "It certainly looks and smells good. Especially since I didn't have breakfast this morning."

"Then dig in." He picked up half of his sandwich but

just held it, continuing to watch her.

"You don't have to tell me twice." Having grown up with three hovering older brothers, one thing Peyton did not have trouble with was eating in front of guys. First, she mashed the overstuffed sandwich with the palm of her hand so she had at least some hope of fitting it into her mouth, then picked up half.

"Nice technique." Drew chuckled.

Peyton paused. The deep rumble was a nice sound.

She forced her attention back to the sandwich, taking her first bite. She was pretty sure her eyes rolled back in her head from the deliciousness, and she totally didn't care that dressing was running down her chin.

This time Drew laughed out loud, and the sound did funny things inside her chest.

"Right?"

"Mmm," was all she could manage.

Then she felt her phone vibrate in her pocket. Her first instinct was to ignore it. Nat must have noticed Peyton had slipped out of the boutique. But she most definitely would have noticed the absence of a certain tall cowboy, and if she put two and two together, she might decide to come looking for them with camera crew in tow. Maybe Peyton had better check her phone. If it was her father, or any other member of her fussy family, she'd call them back later.

With a ridiculous amount of reluctance, Peyton set her sandwich half back in the basket and grabbed for a napkin off the pile Meg had also left.

Drew paused in taking a bite, his stunning eyes intent on

her every move.

Still chewing, she gave him a dismissive, everything's fine wave with one hand while fishing out her phone from her pocket with the other. She glanced at the screen, seeing enough of the text from Sammie to swallow her bite of suddenly dry sandwich with a gulp.

"Trouble?" Drew asked.

Why did he have to be so perceptive?

She shook her head and lied, "Nope. Everything's fine." If fine equaled Natalie on the warpath because Peyton had disappeared with a certain very camera-worthy cowboy. It was only a matter of time before Nat or one of the guys stuck their heads in the diner and spotted them.

Granted, letting Nat film them would be a sure-fire way to show her family how she was letting Dr. Drew dog her steps, with the added benefit of undoubtedly making him uncomfortable. He really didn't seem the reality TV star wannabe type. But the last thing Peyton wanted to do today was be the lone focus of Nat's seemingly endless need for additional camera takes and retakes. It was time to leave.

She looked for Meg. "But I probably should get going. Any chance I can get a to-go box?" She lifted up in her seat so she could pull her credit card from her front jeans pocket, then held it up when Meg turned away from the couple in the booth across from them whose plates she'd just cleared and glanced their way.

Drew held up a staying hand. "No, I've got this." He shifted and pulled his thin wallet from his pocket.

"Because you're the guy?"

"No, because I suggested the diner and recommended the Reuben."

Despite chaffing her sense of independence, she couldn't come up with an argument against his logic, so she nodded.

"Are you going to rejoin the other ladies and the camera crew?" he asked, his gaze keen.

"I am not." She checked to see if Meg was coming, but the waitress had taken the plates she'd cleared back toward the kitchen.

"Are you going back to your trailer at the rodeo grounds?" Was that hope in his voice?

"I am not," she repeated. She mentally consulted the list of Fun Things To Do she'd been compiling since arriving in Pineville, trying to decide which activity would be the best for introducing her babysitter to her way of living. One in particular popped to the forefront, and one corner of her mouth tugged upward. *Oh yeah.*

"What about the meet and greet at two?"

"I'll be back in time." Or she won't. While she was contractually obligated to *Buckin' TV* to ride during the exhibitions the women were putting on at the various rodeos they were visiting, she'd made a point to have flexibility written in to her contract when it came to the other activities Nat planned. It was up to Peyton what she participated in and what she didn't. To a point.

She abruptly asked, "Do you have wheels?"

He sat back. The red faux leather upholstery squeaked beneath his weight. "My truck is parked near the end of Main Street."

Peyton nodded, pleased.

"Why?"

She dodged the specifics with, "My truck gets to spend this week in Pineville's repair shop getting a new transmission."

He opened his mouth, probably to ask her where she planned to go if not back to the rodeo grounds, but Meg arrived at their booth, and Drew instead asked for two take-out boxes and handed over his credit card.

The waitress looked at them with clear speculation but took their still full baskets of food to box up for them.

Peyton rubbed her hands together in anticipation. "That sandwich is going to be so good later."

"Do you have a microwave in your trailer?" Drew asked.

"Yep. And a toaster oven. All the comforts of home."

"Where is home?"

She wiped at her mouth again on the off chance she'd missed some of the delicious sauce and said, "Texas."

"I already know that."

"Outside of The Woodlands, Texas. My family has a ranch there."

He nodded as if he already knew as much. "Where you learned to ride ranch saddle broncs?"

"Exactly."

"School?"

"I went," she quipped, but at the twitch of his eyebrow, she relented and added, "And graduated with a degree in psychology." She'd hoped that not only would she make her family happy by completing her degree instead of simply reveling in her recovery by adventuring, but she'd also come to understand herself better. At least she'd accomplished one of those things. For a little while.

Wanting to shift Drew's attention away from her and her family—though he probably knew more than she'd like, having been hired, or whatever, by her dad—she asked, "And you grew up on the Wright Ranch?"

"I did."

Meg returned with their to-go boxes and Drew's credit card and sales slip for him to sign. He thanked her, and she left with a distinct air of reluctance.

"But you went into medicine instead of rodeo rough stock ranching?" The spark of curiosity over his choice of careers flared to life.

He took the time to return his credit card to his wallet and his wallet to his pocket before answering. "Someone had to," he answered blithely.

Despite knowing exactly how dangerous ranching life could be, she didn't buy it. But she compressed her lips to keep her opinion to herself.

He blew out a heavy breath that let her know she'd failed at hiding her thoughts. His ability to read her was getting dangerous.

Drew said, "My oldest brother Ian runs the ranch, my second oldest brother Liam handles the broncs, and Alec—"

"Who was with you in the arena yesterday, right?"

He inclined his head. "Who was with me in the arena because he is currently pursuing a bull riding career and was attempting to take a practice ride until a couple of daredevil women decided to rile up his bull."

Though more than a little pleased he'd called her and Sammie daredevils instead of just plain stupid, she focused on one particular part of his statement. "Currently? As in temporary?"

"I expect he'll take over the bucking bull program from my grandfather when...well, when he's ready."

Peyton completely understood Drew's hesitancy to put his grandfather's demise to words. Her own beloved grandfather was still a force of nature who seemed impervious to his age. But she knew as well as Drew obviously did that no matter how much they might wish otherwise, even forces of nature eventually had an end.

Not wanting to dwell, she asked, "What about your sister?"

He sat back, and for a second, she feared he was about to ask *Google much?* And she wasn't about to give up Sammie for her flash internet search abilities.

Instead, he said, "She is in the process of taking over her husband's bull program."

"Really?" Peyton couldn't help but be impressed and gratified to hear a man would be willing to let a woman take the lead.

He shrugged as if it was a given. "She has a way with bulls. Especially when they're calves."

If only Peyton had a way with oil wells or pipelines.

No. She rejected the thought. She didn't want to go into the family business. She wanted to experience life. To really live as much and as hard as she could. While she'd escaped any lingering health issues, she was definitely more aware of her mortality than most, and there was still so much that she wanted to do.

To that end, she said, "So your truck is just down the boardwalk?"

"It is. Why?"

"I need you to take me somewhere."

"Back to the rodeo grounds?"

"Eventually." She scooted to the end of the booth and peeked around the edge to check the front of the restaurant. She assumed she would have heard Nat and the crew if they had come through the door but better safe than sorry.

Seeing the coast was clear, she snagged her hat from the seat and boxed sandwich from the table and stood. "Come on, let's go."

"Where?" Drew asked, his deep voice made deeper by suspicion. He grabbed his own hat, pushed his way from the booth, and picked up the white box holding his sandwich. His icy gaze never left hers.

"You'll find out." She winked.

WITH A PARTING wave of his hat to Meg, Drew followed Peyton Halliday, who he was pretty sure his grandfather would call a firebrand, out of the Pineville Diner. Despite his best efforts, he found himself watching her backside and how her long hair bounced in time with her stride. What was wrong with him?

Momentarily blinded by the brightness of the blazing sun once he stepped out of the dimly lit restaurant, he walked right into her back. She'd stopped dead just outside the door. At first, he assumed she was simply waiting for her eyes to adjust to the dramatically different light level, but the moment he was able to see, he realized she was peering one way, then the other, down the boardwalk on both sides of the street.

Being considerably taller and able to see over the parked cars and trucks, Drew was able to immediately spot the dark-haired producer across the street. Nat appeared to be searching the stores across the way for Peyton.

He leaned down and tilted his head so he could whisper in Peyton's ear without knocking their hats off. "Look across the street, to your left, four cars down."

She jolted and knocked the brim of their hats together despite his efforts. They both barely caught them before they came off even as Peyton followed his instructions and looked where he'd directed. Drew knew the moment she saw her producer because she hunched down.

Drew grinned. Pretty sure Peyton wouldn't be able to see over the small SUV directly in front of them, he kept his eyes on the *Buckin' TV* producer as he said, "Nat is heading into the silver jewelry store in three...two...one. Coast is clear."

"Are you sure?"

Her voice came from behind him. Drew turned and saw that Peyton had ducked behind him, using his body to shield her from the view of anyone who might look their way. He'd never seen anything more adorable.

But he felt compelled to say, "You're aware that Nat knows what I look like and why I'd be with you, right?"

"Sammie said she saw you talking with Nat, but I'd hoped she was just asking you if you wanted a chance to be on TV. You being a"—as she straightened, her gaze traveled over him, the gold in her eyes sparkling in the bright sunlight—"cowboy and all."

He laughed and gestured for her to start making their way down the boardwalk toward his truck. "The conversation did start out that way." Despite what he said about being recognizable by Nat, he kept Peyton between himself and the buildings. Hopefully, his body and the parked cars would be enough to block Peyton from being spotted. While he didn't know for certain, he was pretty sure the Halliday family hadn't basically bribed someone from the sports medicine clinic into watching over her so that she would get to be on TV as much as Natalie Polk seemed to want her to be.

She hustled to keep pace with him. It took her nearly two steps to his one, but she didn't complain, instead holding her to-go box beneath one arm and keeping her hat tilted in an attempt to hide her identity. A laughable endeavor considering all that glorious red hair and her white T-shirt with the Dallas Cowboys football team name and logo emblazoned across her chest.

The nearly hypnotizing motion of her breasts beneath the T-shirt had him yanking his gaze away from her and redirecting it across the street to the last business he'd seen Nat enter. He reminded himself he was going to keep things between them clinical, not personal. A challenge, for sure, but Drew was confident he could handle the spitfire and remain detached just fine.

"Where's your truck?"

He looked toward the end of the boardwalk they were quickly approaching and pointed. "It's the black dually parked at the end, there, across the street and in front of the coffee shop."

"Of course. The one with the Wright Ranch logo painted in gold on the doors."

He shrugged. "It's a hand-me-down from my brother, Liam."

"Nice brother."

Thinking of all the times Liam had made him eat dirt, he smirked. "Not really. But after marrying our neighbor, Amanda, he drives Sky High Ranch trucks now."

Drew shifted his box to his other hand and stopped her with a touch on her back as they drew even with where his truck was. "Let's cross here."

Keeping her tucked behind him, he guided her between a dust-coated white truck and a silver sedan as he scanned the boardwalk and the business fronts across from them.

As soon as the traffic and proverbial coast was clear, he said, "Okay, go." He walked briskly across the street, but not so fast that Peyton couldn't keep up. He was strangely gratified when she broke into a trot to draw even with him, again using his body as cover.

They had just reached the back of his truck when a loud commotion came from the specialty candy store three storefronts down from where he'd parked. The Buckin' Babes and the camera crew were leaving the shop in a laughing, jostling scrum of long hair and snug western jeans. Fortunately, they were all turning away from him and Peyton, but just to be safe, he hustled her around to the driver's side of the truck. The dually was more than big enough to hide her from view once they reached the double cab.

He opened the rear door and she practically dove in, sliding her boxed-up sandwich across the seat but remaining crouched low behind the driver's seat.

Shaking his head at the ridiculousness of it all, Drew shut the door behind her, opened the driver's door, and hoisted himself in. He set his to-go box on the front passenger seat.

"Are they still headed in the other direction?" she asked behind him.

He glanced out the passenger window at the gaggle of women and the two men. One guy was balancing a large camera on his shoulder and watching the action through a viewfinder, and the sound guy held a huge, fuzzy microphone over the group as if trying to tempt a bunch of birds with a furry caterpillar.

Drew started the truck with a rumble of the engine and waited a beat to see if anyone turned their way. "No, they're staying put, but thanks to bags of newly purchased chocolate, they're occupied."

"Good. Just go then."

Drew put the gear shift into reverse but didn't take his foot off the brake. "So back to your trailer at the rodeo grounds?" He tried again to make his job as easy as possible.

"Eventually," she said again, probably trying to sound breezy, but considering her current position, she simply sounded a touch demented.

Drew tried to see her in the rearview mirror, but only the crown of her cowboy hat was visible. "Okay. Then where to before *eventually*?"

"Just head out of town. West."

"Yes, ma'am." Drew backed out of the diagonal parking space and slowly made his way back down Main Street. He couldn't help but glance at the cluster of lady bronc riders, who were now slowly making their way along the boardwalk. He locked eyes with Sammie, and she watched him intently as he drove away.

"Will Sammie tell on you?"

"What?"

"Sammie just watched me drive by. Does she know you're with me?"

"Yes."

"Yes, she'll tell on you?" He tried to catch sight of Sammie in his side mirror. Though he didn't know why he cared. He was doing exactly what her family wanted him to do. Nothing could possibly happen to her while she was with him. He wouldn't allow it.

"No, she won't tell on me. She's my friend. But yes, she knows I'm with you. She's the one who texted me that Nat was on the hunt. Can I get up now?"

He was about to say yes when he spotted Natalie standing on the corner of the boardwalk, hands planted on her hips, looking very much like the pissed-off executive producer she was as she stared out at the parking lot of Frank's Groceries. "Give it a sec," he answered instead.

Once he'd turned off Main Street, he said, "Okay, you can sit up now."

She whooped, but instead of just climbing up into the backseat, she scrambled over the center console and picked up his to-go box so she could plop down in the front passenger captain's seat.

She sent him a beaming smile that dried the spit in his mouth as she buckled herself in. "That was excellent. Thanks."

He wasn't about to accept her gratitude until he knew what she was up to. Any woman, hell, anyone, who gleefully climbed on the back of animals like Karen From Finance or, God help him, Red Rum was not to be trusted.

He turned his attention back to the road and again asked, "Where are we going?"

"I want to go check out the mountain."

Drew waved a hand at the lineup of legitimate mountains in front of them as he drove out of town. "I'm afraid you need to be more specific."

"Mt. Bachelor. I've heard a lot about Mt. Bachelor, like how you can drive right up to it."

"You can do more than that. In the winter, you can ski from the very top to pretty much all over the mountain. This time of year, you can bomb down it on mountain bikes." The second the words left his mouth, he immediately regretted them.

"Cool," she said, then laughed at him. "Don't worry, I don't want to go mountain biking. Today."

She laughed again when he shot her a look.

Hoping to dissuade her, he said, "It's almost an hour's drive from here."

"Oh, I'm sure you can get us there faster in this bad boy." She patted the dash.

He could, if he were the speeding type. Which he wasn't. He must have looked like he was ready to turn the truck around and take her back to the rodeo, which he was, because she grew serious. "Honest, I just want to check out the view. Cross my heart."

Drew watched her make an x over the chest he'd swore he wouldn't think about and feared that, promise or not, he just might be in serious trouble with a certain Peyton Halliday and his ability to resist her cute and fiery appeal.

CHAPTER SEVEN

FEELING RIDICULOUSLY PLEASED with herself, Peyton settled back into the plush, tan leather captain's seat in Drew Neisson's big black truck. The early summer, noon-time sun glinted off the gleaming truck's hood and bathed the green irrigated fields and scattered scrub brush in a shimmering glow.

She really loved when things went her way. And ever since leaving the Double H, her family's ranch, to join the cast and crew of the *Buckin' TV* reality—ish—show, things had definitely been going her way.

Even with her family's attempt to hobble her from afar.

She glanced at the handsome profile of the man seated next to her, driving the truck. His square jaw and straight nose were in perfect balance to the white cowboy hat that he wore pulled low on his brow. His emerging blond beard stubble was clearly visible even though it was barely past noon. But it was the long, thick, dark blond lashes framing eyes so light blue they seemed transparent from the side that created a flutter low in her belly. Or maybe it was his full but masculine lips.

He'd remained mostly silent during the drive toward Mt.

Bachelor, which surprised Peyton. Most guys practically burst with questions about why she did whatever she happened to be doing, especially considering who her family was. Invariably, the questions always circled around to her family. And their billions.

But not Drew. Those tempting lips of his remained firmly closed. Maybe because his own grandfather had established a sort of dynasty of his own within the rodeo world. Or maybe because he simply didn't care.

Peyton forced her gaze back to the incredible view of the string of still snowcapped mountains growing closer with each passing mile. She pointed at the very distinct, very tall mountains. "Which one is Bachelor?"

Drew spared her a quick glance, then lifted a finger off the wheel and directed it toward the last peak in the string of mountains. "That's Mt. Bachelor. The next, shorter one is Broken Top, then South Sister, Middle Sister, and North Sister."

She smirked. "The Sisters and the Bachelor?"

"The Three Sisters, to be precise. And Mt. Bachelor, all on his lonesome. And because it's a clear day, on the north end, that's the tip of Mt. Washington and then Mt. Jefferson."

"That's a lot of mountains."

"I consider us blessed." He shrugged.

She nodded. "You are not wrong."

Peyton did her best to take in the view before her. The rugged, high desert landscape, complete with patches of bare, ancient lava rock, gradually gave way to a more forested landscape as they climbed in elevation. Eventually, the mountains were playing peekaboo behind the increasingly thick pine forest of the foothills visible out the truck's front windshield.

Blessed or not, Drew Neisson was nothing more than an unexpected ticket out of the only part of participating on *Buckin' TV* she didn't care for. As much as she loved having the chance to travel the country, meeting new people like the increasingly intriguing cowboy driving her toward her next adventure and, most of all, getting to experience the rush of riding some truly amazing bucking broncs, she wasn't a fan of the often staged, pseudo-real-life activities Natalie Polk cooked up for the lady bronc riders.

Peyton understood Nat had a season's worth of half-hour shows to produce. It couldn't be easy to generate that much content when the actual action only accounted for eight seconds. Peyton didn't begrudge the older woman's attempts to do her job as well as she could. But Peyton was also well aware of why she'd been chosen to be on the show, and she did everything she could to fulfill the *rich girl overcomes illness* storyline by riding to the best of her abilities. And she'd promised herself a long time ago that she wouldn't waste one single second that she'd been blessed with on this earth.

She intended to live.

As if to punctuate the thought, her stomach growled. Loudly.

Drew glanced at her.

Her cheeks heating because she'd been the one to insist

they leave before eating more than a bite of their lunches, she pressed a hand to her belly.

It responded with an even louder grumble.

A corner of Drew's mouth tipped upward. "Feel free to dig into one of those sandwich boxes. Unless you can wait until we get to the West Village Lodge of the Mt. Bachelor ski resort. It's open pretty much year 'round, with food and drinks, and the patio has a really spectacular view."

Because Peyton had no intention of sitting around, enjoying a spectacular view from a boring old patio, she twisted in her seat and reached behind her to grab the to-go box she'd shoved onto the passenger side of the backseat. Once she had it, she turned back around and settled it on her lap. The minute she opened the folded over flaps of the white box, she was assaulted in the best way possible by the heavenly smell of the Reuben and thin, crisp fries.

Looking from the Thousand Island oozing sandwich to the pristine interior of the well-maintained truck cab, she asked, "Are you sure you want me eating this in here?"

Without taking his eyes of the road, Drew gave a silent scoff. "This is a rodeo rough stock ranch truck. It can stand a little Reuben sauce."

Clearly, he hadn't seen her eat enough. "If you say so. Do you want to eat yours?"

"No, I'm good."

She returned her attention to the open box on her lap. Luckily, Meg had stuffed a wad of napkins in the box, so Peyton would be able to contain any mess she would undoubtedly make. She proceeded to devour the sandwich and a substantial amount of fries.

Drew glanced at her approvingly. "You'd get along with my sister. She could have a career as a competitive eater. Especially now that she has a little one to chase after."

"What's your sister's name?" Peyton asked around a mouthful. She couldn't remember if Sammie had mentioned his sister's name when she'd done an internet search on the family, and Drew hadn't told Peyton her name when he'd talked about her helping with her husband's bull program because of her affinity for bull calves.

"Caitlin."

Peyton swallowed the last bite and wiped her mouth with the remaining clean napkin. "And her little one?"

"My niece, Becca. Short for Rebecca. She's named after our mom."

Suddenly Peyton wished she hadn't stopped Sammie from reading what she'd found about his family on the internet. She could always ask him outright about his mom, but then he might want to know about hers, and she wasn't in the mood to share.

"That's very sweet," she said as she set the now empty to-go box at her feet.

"Yeah." The one word held a lot of weight that Peyton couldn't interpret.

She let the subject drop.

They rounded a corner in the four-lane road they'd been traveling on, and Mt. Bachelor appeared before them, a perfect melty ice cream cone of a mountain. As they drove nearer, she could clearly see the lift lines and ski runs branching out in every direction like spider veins.

She squinted and pointed at the very tippy top of the perfectly formed cone of a mountain. "Is there a building on the top?"

"It's the top of the Summit chairlift."

"Meaning you weren't kidding when you said you could ski down from the top of the mountain?"

"I was not. Can't say that I've done it since I graduated from high school, but an awful lot of people who live in Bend do it every day in the winter."

"That's crazy."

"Says the girl from Texas."

She conceded his point with a shrug. "Can we go up there now?"

"No. That particular ski lift only runs in the winter. But do you see that structure halfway up the mountain, there?"

Peyton followed with her gaze where he was pointing. Though it blended in with the rocks it was built upon, she spotted a surprisingly large, low building on a mid-mountain outcropping. "I do."

"That's Pine Martin Lodge. It's open now."

"How do you get there?"

"The Pine Martin lift."

She nodded as if he'd just told her the sky was blue. "Of course. Where do we catch it?"

"We won't need to. The West Village Lodge, at the base of the Pine Martin lift, will be good enough."

Says you.

In her out loud voice, she merely murmured, "Mmm

hmm."

DREW COULDN'T HELP but smile at the excitement and unabashed awe glowing on Peyton's beautiful face as she sat as far forward as his truck's seat belt would allow, seeming to take in every inch of the nine thousand odd foot mountain looming before them. He found himself seeing the mountain anew, appreciating its beauty in a way he couldn't remember doing for a very long time.

As he drove them past the entrances to the Sunrise Lodge, the Junior Race Center, and on to the main West Village Lodge and Nordic Center with the vast parking area between, he explained what each was as best he could. And he couldn't help but get swept up in the wonder of it all.

The acres of parking were mostly empty, though there were a few dozen cars parked in haphazard rows near the ticketing and gift shop building set into the rise that led up to the day use lodge. Drew parked as near as he could to the concrete walkway that zigzagged its way up the slope to the West Village Lodge. The lodge's patio was accessed by heavy duty metal stairs built to withstand the weight of a lot of snow, now melted away except for the highest elevations.

After they climbed from the truck and met in front of the hood, Peyton looked to him, her excitement palpable. "Skiing is closed now, right?"

He looked to the rocky and even grassy slopes above them that seemed impossibly steep without their normal feet upon feet of snow. "Definitely."

She looked at the cars in the lot. "So, all these people are…?"

"Mountain biking, hiking, having lunch at the lodge…" He trailed off and shrugged. "I can think of worse places to spend an early summer day."

Her attention settled on the ticketing and general guest services building nearest them. "I need to use the restroom." She turned and briskly started for the nearest entrance.

He hurried to follow her, figuring he could browse in the gift shop while he waited for her, but Peyton half turned toward him.

"Why don't you go on up to the patio and find us a good place to sit?"

"I can come with you. I'll wait in the shop."

"Please," she scoffed. "I'm not one of those women who can't go to the bathroom by herself. And I can see the patio up there. I won't get lost. Promise."

Peyton Halliday getting lost wasn't what worried him. But aside from buying her weight in knit caps and sunglasses, he couldn't think of any way for her to get herself in trouble. "Okay. See you right up there." He pointed at the stairs leading to the lodge patio and changed direction.

She touched a finger to the brim of her cowboy hat and trotted off to the ticketing and guest services building.

Drew made himself turn away so he wasn't tempted to watch her backside the same way he had her front.

Clinical, not personal.

He shook his head as he started up the path to the day

use lodge's vast concrete patio. He couldn't believe how often he was having to remind himself of something that was normally second nature to him. But Peyton Halliday wasn't the typical patient he would normally see in the clinic. Nothing about this was typical or normal. He was only dogging her heels to secure the chance to improve and sustain the sports medicine clinic. To secure his future. At least, the only future he'd wanted for a very long time.

As Drew climbed the slotted metal stairs leading to the patio, a sense of unease unfurled in his gut. He really shouldn't have allowed her out of his sight. At least not this far. Once he reached the patio, instead of choosing one of the unoccupied tables and chairs to sit at to wait for Peyton, he turned around to go back down the stairs.

And found Peyton at the base of the stairs ready to climb them with sheaves of paper clutched in one hand.

She glanced up, saw him, and raised her coppery eyebrows. "No tables?"

He hesitated. Did he tell her there were plenty of tables, but he hadn't trusted her to be on her own?

She waved her own question away. "It doesn't matter. Turns out we don't have time to sit down."

The hair on the back of Drew's neck stood on end. "What—?"

"Come on!" Peyton waved him down with the papers she held and skirted the stairs. "You can sign your release at the yurt."

"My *release*?" The unease in his gut exploded into full-on dread. "Peyton!" he called after her, but she was already out of sight. Banging his way down the metal stairs, he yelled, "What did you do?"

She didn't respond. When he reached the bottom of the stairs, using the handrail to slow his momentum and swing himself in the direction she'd disappeared, he spotted her jogging toward the brown canvas yurts erected atop wooden platforms.

Without turning, she yelled, "Come on, Dr. Neisson! Your zip line awaits!"

Drew stopped so fast dirt and gravel kicked up as if he were a kid who'd just bombed down the hill trails on a mountain bike. *Zip line?*

His gaze leapt to the yurts Peyton was practically skipping toward and the additional platforms on either side of them. One was a few feet off the ground with a pair of cables stretching only a couple dozen feet. A practice line? The other platform that was farther away from the canvas structures was significantly taller, and the thick cables attached to it led somewhere up the mountain and looked very much like power lines.

At that moment, the air was filled with a high-pitched buzzing, almost whining sound, followed by distinctly feminine shouts of "*Woohoo!*"

Drew followed the sound just in time to spot two women riding the zip line down at shockingly fast speeds. Drew's heart lurched into his throat, believing there was no way the women would be able to survive hitting the literal end of the line, until he realized part of the whining sound he was hearing was a brake of some sort being applied to the cable.

By the time the riders reached the platform, where Drew now noticed two employees waiting beneath each cable, the women had slowed their mad descents to gentle glides that the employees were able to easily halt. They were eased to their feet and released from the carriage.

They promptly high-fived each other.

Drew looked back at Peyton and found her jumping up and down in shared jubilation.

He was so screwed.

She jumped in his direction, caught sight of him just standing there, and waved him toward her again.

Would her family pull the clinic funding because he let her go zip-lining?

Would they pull it because he stopped her, but she went back to the rodeo and climbed on another rank bronc or, God help him, a bull and became seriously hurt?

He looked up the mountain, for the first time noticing the series of towers and connecting cables. No matter how fast the descent, it would take some time to gear up, ride the Pine Martin chair lift up to midmountain where it appeared the first and highest tower had been erected. Maybe Peyton would miss her slotted ride in the exhibition tonight.

It might just be worth it.

Peyton had made it to the steps leading up to the yurts and turned to holler at him. "Come on, Drew! Hurry! Our group is up next!"

Deciding his odds of stopping her were pretty thin unless he resorted to a physical intervention in the form of tossing her over his shoulder and carrying her back to his truck,

Drew broke into a trot to appease her.

By the time he reached the stairs, Peyton had already hurried up them and handed the papers she held to an employee, then pointed at Drew and spoke excitedly.

The young man, wearing a Grip It and Zip It hooded sweatshirt, separated one paper and held it and a pen out to Drew. "You have to sign this, sir."

Assuming it was an *if I die, I won't sue* form, Drew nodded and mounted the stairs. Slanting a look at Peyton, who smiled beguilingly back at him and made his gut clench with unexpected desire, he initialed and signed where required. Hopefully, no one noticed his hand shaking.

The kid took the paper and pen back and asked them both to stand on a scale, explaining that they needed exact weights to match each rider with the proper harness system.

Peyton didn't hesitate, stepping on the scale, then laughed and patted her tummy. "Reuben baby."

The kid sent her a panicked look, and Drew rushed to reassure him. "She's talking about her lunch."

Belatedly getting her joke, the kid released his breath and directed them into the yurt where they found additional employees showing three other couples how to step into and tighten their harnesses, don helmets, and secure backpacks holding the carriage that would attach to the zip-line cable. Once Drew and Peyton were matched with the proper equipment, everyone was required to watch a short video on how to sit back in the harness and operate the hand brake on the carriage.

Peyton could barely contain herself, bouncing on the

toes of her boots. Drew found himself being sucked in by her enthusiasm to the point that when it was finally time for them to take their practice ride on the very short and very low zip line, he was raring to go also.

He didn't even begrudge her "Yeeha!" when she launched herself off the practice platform. While he had serious concern about where the harness's padded thigh loops met in his crotch, he couldn't deny that riding the line was fun.

After everyone had a chance to practice, the group was led to the chairlift that had been fit with special racks to carry mountain bikes up the mountain. He and Peyton were seated on a chair meant for four, but he made sure she sat close.

Seemingly unconcerned by the ground dropping away from them, she hooked an arm around his. "Thank you for doing this with me. When I read about it online, I knew I had to find a way to do it while I'm here."

"I'm sure Natalie would have loved to get you and the other ladies on camera doing something like this. Talk about a camera-worthy setting." He extended his free hand to the mountain rising above them, covered with fresh grass and alpine flowers where there weren't dirt trails, crags of volcanic rock, and patches of snow clinging stubbornly to highest or shadiest points.

Peyton shook her head. "No. This kind of thing is strictly for me."

"Is that why I was given this assignment? So you'd have a way to do the extracurricular activities you want to do?"

She looked away from him. "No. That is not why you were given this assignment."

Drew waited for her to elaborate, but she didn't.

Instead, she twisted on the padded lift seat to look behind them. Drew couldn't help but pin the arm that she'd wrapped around his tight against his body. It was a long way down, and the rocks below them deadly.

"Wow," she exclaimed. "Now that's a view."

Drew found himself appreciating the beauty of the landscape in a way he hadn't for a very long time. When he looked back down at her, he found her watching him. Her light hazel eyes glowed molten in the sunlight.

"Thank you, Drew. Seriously. Thank you."

He swallowed hard but had to settle for a simple nod in acknowledgment. She was so damn pretty. And earnest. And the temptation to lean close and kiss her was palpable.

He was so screwed.

CHAPTER EIGHT

AFTER CLIMBING UP to the first zip line launch platform with Drew, Peyton turned in a complete circle so she wouldn't miss any of the glorious vista that seemed to go on forever. She could have stood there a long time appreciating the view, but there were thrills to be had.

After the operator attached her trolley and harness to the line, Peyton lifted her feet off the first wood and concrete launch platform and settled her weight on the harness anchored behind her thighs. The same sort of buzzing excitement she experienced right before nodding for the bucking chute gate to be pulled open zinged through her. Only this time without the chaser of fear.

With both hands on the trolley's brake control handle, she leaned back to be able to see around the young woman operator to where Drew was being attached to the cable next to her.

"You ready, Dr. Drew?"

"And if I'm not?"

The operator paused, glancing at Drew's face.

He closed his eyes and gave a quick shake of his head to let her know he didn't mean it.

Peyton grinned. She'd known he'd be game. He wouldn't have taken on the challenge of riding herd on someone like her if he weren't. The guy was starting to grow on her.

When the operator gave them the good to go, Peyton said, "Race you, Doc!" She pulled down on the hand brake to release the trolley from the cable, hitched herself forward enough to start the trolley along the thick cable as they'd been taught during the training, and away she went. They didn't call this zip-lining for nothing.

"Wooohooo!" Peyton exclaimed as she quickly gained speed until she was going so fast her eyes teared up from the brisk alpine air rushing by.

A masculine "Yeah!" sounded next to her, and she turned in time to see Drew blast by her through her watery vision. His much larger body obviously generated more momentum than hers. Every competitive fiber in her, which she already knew to be pretty much all of her fibers, screamed for her to catch up and pass him. But gravity was in charge at the moment.

As they approached the large *slow* sign on the ground, she heard Drew apply the hand brake to his trolley, gradually slowing his descent.

Peyton didn't, continuing at full speed until she flew past him. *Yes.*

"Peyton!" she heard him yell from somewhere behind her.

Judging the distance remaining between herself and the platform, where the operator was frantically signaling her to slow with flapping arms, Peyton pushed up on the brake. A little at first, but as the platform rushed toward her and the operator braced himself to catch her, she jammed the brake upward with all her might.

With a whirring scream, Peyton's trolley brake caught hold, and she arrived at the platform under control.

Mostly.

Her trolley hit the huge, thick metal spring with a very loud, and very embarrassing, *clank*, stopping her with a jolt that was mitigated by the lanky young man who caught her by the waist.

Peyton gave him an apologetic smile as he lowered her to her feet and released her trolley from the cable. She told him, "Wow, you're brave. Good thing I didn't kick you in the face." She lifted a booted foot.

"I have tons of practice." He winked at her.

Drew arrived at the platform, under complete control. At least under control of his speed of descent. His temper, not so much. "Peyton! What the hell?"

She winked back at the operator. "Oops."

He gave a *what can you do* shrug and tucked her trolley into her backpack for the walk over to the next launch tower.

The minute Drew had been freed of the cable, he stomped toward her. The other operator, a young woman not much taller than Peyton, followed on tippy-toes so she could tuck his trolley into his matching black backpack.

"I know you saw the sign, Peyton. Why didn't you slow down?" His ice-blue eyes were again filled with the heat she was starting to really like.

"Because we were racing, silly." Peyton headed for the stairs down from the landing platform and the path to the next launching platform. Over her shoulder, she said, "I won, in case you didn't notice."

His frustrated groan made her smile. Who knew he'd turn out to be so much fun?

As they walked the twenty feet or so to the next tall, poured concrete launch tower, obviously built to withstand the harsh winter conditions so far up the mountain, Peyton asked Drew, "You thought that was fun, right?"

"Expecting to see you splat into a concrete wall like a bug on a windshield was a real hoot," he answered sourly.

She laughed. "Oh, come on. Didn't you see that fine young gentleman ready and waiting to catch me?"

Drew snorted. "I'm pretty sure he was shitting himself watching you hurtling toward him, squealing like a mad woman."

"I was not squealing. I've never squealed in my life."

"If you say so." He waved for her to precede him up the stairs to the next launch platform.

She laughed again, a bubble of happiness growing to the point of exploding in her chest. This was a good day.

And when she was flying down the next section of zip line, she told herself that out of consideration for the poor zip-line employee waiting at the end of the line, she was ready to apply the brake when told by the huge *slow* sign that appeared among the volcanic rock. But when her momentum swung her legs toward Drew, she saw him keeping pace with her on their descent with a look of either worry or appreciation on his face, she really couldn't tell. She found herself pushing up on the brake until her trolley whined out of consideration for him.

Drew must have slowed, also, because they arrived at the landing platform together. The smile he sent her completely derailed her brain. The operator had to tell her twice to put her feet down so she could be detached from the cable.

Okay, so he was a handsome guy. A very handsome guy. But she'd spent her entire life around handsome guys. Drew shouldn't be any different. She just had to keep telling herself as much.

They walked down the stairs from the landing tower together and headed toward the next, and last, launching platform.

Picking her way over the loose rocks, Peyton said, "This is fun. Don't you think this is fun?"

Drew grunted.

Peyton glanced up at him to see if it was a good grunt or a bad grunt. The corners of his mouth were curled upward in a definite smile. A sneaky smile, but still a smile.

A good grunt. She felt like skipping.

They rounded a large boulder, and instead of skipping, Peyton abruptly stopped. Before her was the most magnificent view she'd ever seen. Snow-topped mountains, some smaller than the one they were currently working their way down and other, much larger peaks appeared stunningly close. The blue of the sky was so blue, the white snow gleamed, the water in puddle-like lakes sparkled in the sun, and the green of the forests covering the lower hills was the most vibrant she'd ever seen.

She threw out a hand to stop Drew. "Quick, get my phone out of my backpack pocket. Please?"

"Yes, ma'am." He stepped behind her and moved her ponytail out of the way by sweeping it over her shoulder. His fingers brushed along her neck and sent delicious little shivers down her spine. Her breath froze, and she found herself wanting more.

Which was stupid as hell. Drew was a doctor. She didn't do doctors. On so many levels.

But he merely fished her phone out of the zippered, smaller pocket of the black backpack and stepped away.

"What a sight," she breathed out.

When he moved around her to hand the phone over, he was smiling outright.

Her gaze hung up on his now even more handsome face. Drew Neisson had one hell of a smile. But he wasn't any different from all the other handsome cowboys she knew, she reminded herself.

Nevertheless, she still found herself saying, "You should do that more," as she took her phone from him.

"Do what?"

"Smile." She touched the screen of her phone and accessed the camera app. Moving away from him to better frame the photo, she said, "You have a very winning smile."

"Winning?" He sounded skeptical.

Tempting, actually. "Yes, winning."

Again with the grunt.

Peyton found herself smiling as she took several amazing

photos.

She heard the telltale sound of a photo being taken behind her and turned to see Drew just lowering his smartphone. He'd slipped his backpack off to get his own phone out.

He shrugged. "It is a pretty view."

Heat blossomed in her chest and spread up her neck to her face. She had no idea if it was caused by pleasure or embarrassment.

Drew gestured her toward him. "Come here. I'll put your phone back in the zip pocket. It'd be a shame for you to lose it now."

As she went to him, he bent to replace his own phone, then straightened to take her phone. She turned and allowed him to secure her phone in the backpack she still wore. She could have sworn his hand lingered on her neck and shoulder when he moved her ponytail again. The first time had probably been accidental, but this time, his touch had seemed more purposeful. She shivered as she stepped away, and he was forced to retrieve and don his own backpack.

Peyton was suddenly overheated. How could the sun have grown so hot so fast?

Knowing that careening down a mountain while dangling from a cable was a sure way to cool off, Peyton wasted no time getting up the next launch tower. Luckily, Drew kept up.

The last leg of the zip-line tour was the longest, steepest, and fastest. Peyton couldn't wait.

And judging from the look on Drew's face as their trolleys were being attached to the cable and they were attached to the carriage, he was anticipating the ride with the same sort of excitement.

A ridiculous amount of self-satisfaction swelled throughout Peyton.

She'd known she could get Dr. Button-down to loosen up and enjoy living.

DREW PUSHED UP on the trolley hand brake to slow his descent enough to keep him even with the hooting and hollering beautiful redhead riding the zip line a little under seven feet away from him. Just the sight of her, feet kicking and long red ponytail streaming behind her, made him smile.

She really was something.

Though they had been instructed, repeatedly, to keep both hands on the brake at all times, when Peyton saw him looking her way, she released the brake with one hand to point at him as she let loose another long and loud "Woooo!" including him in her revelry.

Normally, seeing someone put themselves at risk would send him into British nanny mode, but there was something about Peyton's brand of recklessness, at least when he knew she was safely strapped into a three-point harness, that loosened something in his chest. Something that had had a vise grip on him since he'd been a child, lingering unseen in the corner of his mother's sickroom.

But loosened did not equal gone. And considering the

future he'd always wanted was dependent on him keeping her safe from harm, any kind of harm, he yelled, "Both hands on the brake, Peyton!"

She fist-pumped instead.

He was about to yell at her again when they passed over the *slow* sign propped up on the ground, and Peyton dutifully grabbed hold of the brake with both hands and pushed up to slow her descent.

Good girl.

He found himself grinning when he reached the platform.

He looked to Peyton, and she pointed at him again. "Ha! I knew it. You're having fun."

"I'm just happy you didn't slam into that big metal coil and embarrass us again."

"I wasn't embarrassed," she retorted.

"That's okay. I was embarrassed enough for both of us."

She laughed, obviously not buying it. "Poor Dr. Drew."

He realized he was grinning again. But he still had to keep her safe.

As they walked down the stairs of the last landing pad, he lifted her backpack up off her shoulders. "Unfasten this so I can carry it."

She glanced over her shoulder at him. "I've carried it all the way down the mountain. I'm pretty sure I can manage this last leg." She gestured to the elevated yurts about thirty feet away where they would return their gear and reclaim their belongings.

"I know you can." He'd seen her successfully ride Karen

From Finance. He was pretty sure Peyton Halliday could carry any load she set her mind to shouldering. "But I want to carry it for you. My masculinity demands it."

She turned toward him, her beautiful smile wide. "Being a fan of your brand of masculinity, who am I to deny it?" She pulled her chin back and blinked as if stunned by what she'd said.

Had she really meant to say she was a fan of his masculinity? The notion actually made his chest puff up a little.

But then her smile broadened, and she reached up to unfastened the clasp holding the backpack secure over her chest. Drew's gaze automatically went to how the letters on her Cowboys shirt were squished together, among other things, leaving just the *C* and *b* visible until she released the clasp.

He held his hand out for the backpack as she shrugged it off.

"My hero." She sent him an exaggerated smile that scrunched her face up in the most adorable way.

The girl definitely had cojonas.

He liked it.

And he also knew the only way he would keep her from accepting any challenge that came her way was to keep her busy doing safer things.

He took the backpack from her. "I live to serve."

"Is that why you became a doctor?"

"No."

She stopped abruptly and met his eyes.

He hadn't meant to answer so sharply. But he'd told her

the truth.

He pulled his gaze from the concerned glow of her hazel eyes and looked toward the day lodge. "Seeing as my Reuben has been sitting in a hot truck for a couple of hours, you game for grabbing a bite to eat here?"

She snuck a peek at her watch. She was obviously calculating how much time they had until the women's exhibition rides before tonight's official start of the rodeo. Drew knew exactly how much time they had.

The exact amount of time he needed to waste.

"Sure." Her bright smile was back.

It struck Drew that this particular smile of hers might not be genuine. Interesting.

He chewed on the prospect as they climbed the stairs to the yurt platform and placed the backpacks containing their trolleys in the designated bins after retrieving their cell phones and Drew's truck keys from the packs' zippered pocket. The helmets went in a different bin and their harnesses in another.

As a bronc rider, he knew she had exceptional balance, but he couldn't help himself from offering her a hand to help her remain steady as she stepped out of her harness. She accepted his help, sliding her hand into his. Her hand was small, calloused, and strong. He liked the way it felt within his.

The zip-line employee who'd taken their paperwork when they'd first arrived brought their cowboy hats to them, having retrieved them from the cubby shelf they'd left them in.

Drew released Peyton's hand so she could take her hat and plant it on her head. She did so without looking at him.

After tipping the staff, Drew followed Peyton back toward the lodge. Her attention appeared to be on the mountain looming above them, but he had the distinct impression her thoughts were elsewhere.

When they reached the bottom of the metal stairs leading to the vast patio, Peyton stopped. "Um, would it be okay if we just hit a drive-thru? I'll buy."

Drew hesitated. A fast-food drive-thru would not consume the amount of time he needed to waste to make her miss her exhibition ride. He pointed up the stairs. "They have some pretty great sandwiches here, too." He was counting on her enjoyment of the Reuben to sway her. Pretty lame, but he couldn't think of anything else quickly enough.

Peyton reached out and touched a hand to his forearm. "I really need to get back, Drew." She gave him a gentle squeeze. "But this was a lot of fun. Thank you for doing it with me. And for bringing me all the way here." She slid her hand away, but he could still feel the warmth of her touch.

He automatically said, "You're welcome." All the while thinking that he hadn't exactly had any choice.

And aside from physically restraining her, he couldn't keep her away from the rodeo. Not in this day and age of rideshares. Maybe there was another way.

"Okay, then." He gestured toward the parking lot. "Let's get you back to Pineville."

He allowed her to walk ahead of him, taking his phone

from his pocket and texting Liam with what he considered a simple request. He was tucking his phone back in his pocket when it rang. He looked at the caller ID. Liam.

Peyton turned back toward him, but he waved her on, clicking the button on his key fob to unlock the truck. As soon as she'd increased the distance between them, he answered the call.

"Liam."

"What do you mean, switch Peyton Halliday's horse out?"

"Just what I texted you. Switch out whichever horse she drew this morning and replace it with a nag."

"We don't own any nags, Drew."

"You know what I mean, Liam. I need you to make sure Peyton Halliday is matched with a horse that won't hurt her."

Liam's sigh was long and loud through the phone. "I'll see that she rides Mustard Gas."

Relief washed over Drew. "Thank you, Liam. I owe you."

"Damn straight—wait…Peyton Halliday. Isn't she the one who rode Karen From Finance?"

"Yes."

"Then why are you worried—"

"I'll explain it all later. Will you still make sure she's matched with Mustard Gas?"

"I will. But I'll expect that explanation."

"You'll get it. Thanks, Liam."

"You bet. Talk to you later."

Drew clicked off and returned his phone to his pocket. When he reached his truck in the vast parking lot, he found Peyton leaning against the front bumper.

"I unlocked the doors…"

"I know. But it turns out Reuben is a stinky fellow."

"Sorry. I was afraid of that."

"Is everything okay?"

"Yeah. Why?"

"The phone call?"

"Oh, yes. Everything's fine." He almost told her he was checking in with Doc at the clinic, but he couldn't say the words. It was one thing to arrange for a tamer horse for her exhibition ride, and another to out and out lie to her.

Hopefully he could at least keep her safe.

CHAPTER NINE

S TANDING OVER THE bucking chute, Peyton rubbed her gloved hands together in nothing short of glee as she waited for no less than Liam Neisson himself to ready the bucking strap on the palomino bronc she was slated to ride. His thickly muscled shoulders moved and flexed beneath his chambray shirt. Even bent over the bucking chute, he looked bigger than Drew, but there was no doubting the family resemblance.

Not only had she been lucky enough to arrive back from her and Drew's zip-line adventure in time to ride, but the horse she'd drawn that morning before they'd headed into town had been switched out for this one. Which wasn't unusual. These broncs were considered equine athletes, and just like any athlete they sometimes suffered injuries or developed issues that could only be healed with rest.

What was unusual, or at least unexpected, was a horse being replaced by a Wright Ranch bronc. Peyton couldn't believe her luck. A Wright Ranch bronc named Mustard Gas would surely give her a wild ride.

First the exhilaration of literally zipping down a beautiful mountain, capped off by a pulse-pounding eight-second ride on another Wright Ranch bronc. Definitely a great day. She purposefully ignored the little voice in her head that whispered that it had also been a great day because she'd spent it with a certain cowboy doctor.

She was not even going to think about that. In no small part because he was only following her around because her family had hired him. He considered her an assignment. There was nothing remotely personal between them. And there wouldn't be. She didn't need a man to complete her.

Liam fixed blue eyes a shade darker than Drew's on her, running an unmistakably speculative gaze over her.

Had Drew told his brother about his *assignment?*

"You ready?" Liam asked in a voice that shared the same deep timbre as his brother's.

She pushed aside her suspicion that Liam knew Drew had been tasked with being her keeper. He wasn't the first stock contractor to give her the wall eye. No way did they want to believe little 'ol her could successfully ride one of their big bad broncs.

She gave him a big fat smile. "Ready, willing, and able."

A blond brow twitched upward beneath his black cowboy hat.

Peyton redirected her attention to climbing aboard Mustard Gas, who instantly began snorting and flicking his pale cream tail. Doing her best to keep her excitement and anticipation in check, Peyton settled into the saddle, pushed the stirrups as far forward as she could, and leaned back with the bucking rope held high in one hand and wrapped the other around the saddle horn, a concession allowed for her gender. With one last glance at Drew's brother, watching her as he held the bucking strap at the ready to cinch it tight when the horse left the chute, Peyton nodded.

The chute gate was pulled open and Mustard Gas leapt sideways, clearing the chute and kicking out against the tightening of the bucking strap. Peyton braced for the next explosive kick or leap, but the bronc only gave a series of half-hearted bucks. Each kick of his back legs was punctuated by a very loud, very distinct sound.

It hit Peyton then. Mustard Gas hadn't been given his name because his bucking style was deadly. He received the name for more literal reasons. Mustard Gas was one flatulent, stinky horse.

Being in no jeopardy whatsoever of getting bucked off, Peyton held on as she held her breath against the very noxious cloud forming around the horse until the buzzer sounded. By the time the pickup riders drew even with them, the bronc was placidly, but still musically, trotting along. Her ride score, half of which was earned by her mount, was going to be garbage. Very, very smelly garbage.

One of the pickup riders easily plucked her from the saddle, reined his unflappable horse to a stop, and set her on the ground.

"Here's some fresh air for you, ma'am." He didn't even try to hide his amusement. She'd been right about Mustard Gas being aptly named.

Starting the seemingly mile-long trudge back to the chutes, she caught sight of Drew on the catwalk patting his brother Liam's shoulder.

That's what the phone call up on the mountain had been about. Drew had arranged for her to be matched with a bronc the complete opposite of the rank and dangerous Karen From Finance. The same sort of calmness she always experienced when her family found a new way to trap her indoors and lock away the silver platters she'd used to sled down the front stairs on filled her.

Well played, Dr. Drew. Well played.

Too bad for him she was good at this game. Because when life took away the silver platters, it was time to break out the laundry baskets.

A SINKING FEELING akin to launching himself off the zip line settled in the pit of Drew's stomach as he watched Peyton walk back toward the catwalk, her well-worn chaps flapping around her shins, her head down. The wide, flat brim of her cowboy hid her face from view, but there was something about the way she tromped through the loose dirt of the arena, taking the long way to steer clear of the mounted drill team charging around the arena to entertain the crowd between rides, that set off alarm bells in his head.

Beside him, Liam said, "I'm thinking you might have just made a tactical error with that one, little brother."

"Probably. But it couldn't be helped. As you said, we don't own any nags."

Liam turned to look at him. "Care to explain?"

Not really, but Drew knew Liam wouldn't let the matter

slide. He glanced around the busy catwalk to see if anyone was paying any attention to them. No one was. The camera crew and the other lady bronc riders were helping the next woman set up on the bronc one chute down from him and Liam.

Figuring they wouldn't be overheard, Drew said, "Her family has offered Doc a huge chunk of change for the sports medicine clinic program."

"A huge chunk?"

Drew nodded. "Yes. Enough for the upgrade it needs and to provide a buffer if any of the rodeos can't fully afford the program in a given year. It seems they aren't thrilled with Peyton risking her neck riding broncs. Among other things."

"But if she covered Karen From Finance, she must be good at bronc riding."

Drew could only shrug. It didn't really matter why her family didn't want her in harm's way, only that they had the power to affect his future.

"So, they're using their financial pull to get you to play nursemaid?"

Everyone assumed Liam was nothing more than the muscle of the family, but Drew knew he was obviously so much more. The guy could spot a good horse a mile away, and he could effortlessly settle the rowdiest bronc.

Drew nodded again. "Bingo."

"Why not just get Grandfather to foot the bill for the clinic so you're not beholden to anyone outside of the family?"

"That was my first thought when Doc told me what my

new *assignment* was."

"And?"

"And Grandfather said no. He wants me to fulfill my commitment to the clinic and its patron."

"Does she know?" Liam tilted his head toward Peyton down in the arena.

Fully aware he'd made a ham-fisted mistake when he'd first approached her, Drew lifted his hat from his head so he could run a hand through his hair. "Yes." He replaced his hat and gave the brim a tug.

Liam grunted, redirecting his attention to the woman nearing the arena fencing to the left of the bucking chutes. "Well, if she is what I'd assume to be said patron's golden child, you best find a way to smooth things over. She doesn't have to be a genius to figure out that you had her mount switched."

Drew had been fully prepared to weather the storm of Peyton's anger when he'd first texted Liam. Drew knew from her excitement after riding Karen From Finance how much she valued the challenge of a rank mount. And he was starting to get a feel for how much she disliked being managed in any way. Her avoidance of activities arranged by her executive producer Nat a case in point.

Maybe the small smile he could now see teasing at her mouth was simply because she was, from what he could tell, a generally good-natured person and was taking in stride being paired with a disappointing mount.

Or maybe she was plotting her revenge.

A cold chill passed over Drew.

At that exact moment, Peyton looked up toward the catwalk, and her gaze collided with his. There was no mistaking the distinct glint of purpose in her warm honey eyes.

Yep. She was pissed.

Drew realized he didn't like being responsible for her anger even more than he disliked the thought of whatever revenge she might cook up.

Liam slapped him on the back. "Good luck with that." His brother chuckled as he moved away down the catwalk.

Fortunately, thanks to their sister and her best friend Amanda, who was now Liam's wife, Drew had an idea or two about how to handle a female with her hackles up. The first and foremost tactic would be to begin and end each sentence with *yes, ma'am*.

He continued to watch Peyton as she reached the metal arena fencing and removed her hat to step through. Her glorious long red hair, still in the low ponytail she'd confined it to so it didn't catch in the zipline trolley, fell over her shoulder as she bent to step through the fence rails.

Something stirred low in Drew's belly. Something he was starting to become accustomed to when around Peyton. He studiously ignored it. He didn't have the time for what might become of his attraction to her. Nor the inclination. She was a risk taker, and he was the poster child for risk adverse.

Though he knew she would be making her way back up to the catwalk to provide assistance to her fellow lady bronc riders, several of whom were watching him and Liam with blatant speculation, Drew made his way to the stairs and hurried down to meet Peyton. If she intended to chew his head off here and now, he'd rather she did it away from the catwalk and out of earshot of the camera crew and other riders.

At the bottom of the stairs, he once again found himself standing between her and her access to the catwalk.

Her attention was clearly on replacing her hat to her head, so Peyton had to pull up short to keep from running into him.

She looked up and smiled. "Oh, hey," she said with far more nonchalance than he'd expected.

Alarm bells went off in his head. Was this the calm before the storm?

"Did you see that?"

By *that* he assumed she meant her ride on Mustard Gas. "I did," he admitted cautiously.

"Talk about a real...dud."

Drew thought for sure she'd been about to say *stinker*. Mustard Gas had definitely earned his name from a young age. Drew was pretty sure Liam kept the gelding around for comedy relief.

"Lucky for me, I had an amazing ride yesterday. I might still be okay in the scoring."

Drew tucked his chin at her lack of heat. Maybe he'd misread her anger after the ride. "I thought this was an exhibition."

"It is. But we're all still competitors. Just because the women's scores only officially count while riding on the circuit back in Texas doesn't change things when we're riding together elsewhere. We still keep track."

Guilt for meddling with her ride crept up the back of Drew's neck. But just like his growing attraction to her, he ignored it. The end of protecting the clinic's future justified whatever means he found himself forced to employ.

He nodded vaguely. "Makes sense."

"Well, I'd better get up there and help the other girls who still have rides coming up. Then after that, I'm going to have to go back to my trailer and hit the hay. Turns out zipping down a mountain is exhausting. A heck of a lot more exhausting than riding Mustard Gas." She emphasized the word *gas*, then practically snorted. She batted her thick eyelashes up at him. "Will I see you tomorrow?"

Utterly confused by her seemingly good mood, he stammered, "Uh…uh, sure."

"Good. Maybe we can find something else fun to do before I have to ride." She squarely met his gaze, and there was no mistaking the hard glint in her hazel eyes.

And there it was.

She was indeed pissed. And she undoubtedly had a plan to make him pay. His stomach churned as he tried to think of all the possibilities, but he knew there was no way he'd be able to prepare himself for what someone like Peyton Halliday might cook up.

His only choice would be to wait and see.

PEYTON HADN'T BEEN lying when she'd told Drew Neisson she intended to return to her trailer after the women's exhibition. Nat hadn't been happy about Peyton not only missing the meet and greet, but once again skipping the hanging-out-on-the-fence-ogling-the-cowboys part of the evening. But there wasn't much Nat could do about it. Peyton and her poor-little-rich-girl storyline had the potential for high ratings once the show aired for Nat to risk Peyton quitting the show altogether.

Peyton had been lying about being so tired she intended to hit the hay, however. The need for revenge was burning too hotly in her veins for her to rest. Instead, after the women's exhibition, she returned to her trailer, peeled off her grimy clothes in favor of her flannel sleep pants and cotton T-shirt, turned out all but her reading light, climbed into bed, and promptly fired up her computer to recheck things to do in the Central Oregon high desert.

She was seriously considering making reservations to rent a surf board so she'd be able to attempt to ride the manmade rapids in the Deschutes River where it ran through nearby Bend when her skin prickled. She set her laptop on the bed and climbed to her knees to peer out the small window above the sleeping nook in the little trailer. After pulling aside the curtain, she saw nothing unusual in the spillover light from the rodeo arena. With the rodeo still going, the noise of the crowd drowned out any sound that would have been enough out of place to draw her attention.

She was about to let the curtain drop when she noticed a tall, broad-shouldered cowboy loitering across the graveled thruway between the rows of competitors' campers, trailers, and RVs that made up the temporary village.

Drew Neisson.

His strong, tapered back was turned toward her, and his head was up, as if he was trying to discern what was happening within the arena. Did it grate on him that he couldn't be leaning on the railing, watching with a trained eye for the regrettable but inevitable injuries that occurred within a rodeo arena? He seemed the type who wouldn't want to slack on his job in any way, shape, or form.

But obviously her father had been clear about what Drew's job was as long as she was in his neck of the woods.

Peyton let the curtain drop and sat back on her bed. Not only had he crashed their shopping trip and had his brother switch her bronc, but he had the nerve to stand around outside her trailer. Was he making sure she didn't slip out and…do what? Pick up some ax murderer to bring back to her little trailer?

Anger and a frustration born of years of being smothered sent her bolting from the bed and stomping to the door of her trailer. But her hand froze on the latch. Confronting Drew now would not provide her with the payback she burned for.

She forced herself to retreat back to her bed and resettle her computer on her lap. If Drew wanted to play sentinel, then let him.

Despite a tingling awareness that refused to subside, Peyton kept scrolling through activities available within a reasonable distance of the rodeo grounds. She clicked on a promising link and immediately knew she'd found the perfect revenge for the substitution of Mustard Gas for the bronc she'd originally drawn from the hat. She made notes of the necessary information and shut down her computer.

Regardless of how much she wanted to peek out the window again to see if her babysitter was still hanging around outside her trailer, Peyton forced herself to turn off the light above her bed and crawl beneath the covers. She needed to get to sleep because she fully intended to be up, ready, and waiting on the clinic's doorstep when Drew arrived for work tomorrow morning.

Then she'd scare the living daylights out of him.

CHAPTER TEN

T HE NEXT MORNING, Drew yawned for the third time before he'd even left his truck to walk the short distance from where he'd parked his truck and the clinic's door on the other side of the trailer. He was exhausted and couldn't fully wake up, despite the fact he'd downed the majority of a pot of coffee before he'd left the Wright Ranch main house, much to the annoyance of his father who had a month's worth of ranch financials to wade through today.

After spending just one day with Peyton Halliday, he was wrung out. Hurtling down a mountain, making sure she survived another bronc ride unharmed, then following her back to her trailer and lurking around outside, making sure she didn't slip back out and try whitewater rafting at night was exhausting. But he had to know for sure that she'd been telling the truth when she'd said she was turning in. And as long as a light remained on in her little trailer, he hadn't dare leave, even though a rodeo he should have been working was in full swing.

Doc Tracer had assured Drew that he had it handled, reminding Drew once again that he'd been tending to injured rodeo folk for longer than Drew had been alive.

Nevertheless, Drew's stress level had climbed with each exclamation, with each gasp erupting from the crowd in the stands that he could clearly hear while standing in the shadows across from Peyton's trailer. But the only thing he could do was tell himself Doc was right, he certainly was more than capable of tending any injury that might occur in the arena.

And with the future of the clinic, Drew's future, potentially contingent on how well he kept Peyton safe, he would skulk outside her trailer all night if necessary.

Drew rounded the back of the clinic trailer and nearly missed a step at the sight of Peyton lounging on the folding steps below the closed clinic door. She'd propped her back against the door and had stretched her legs out in front of her, crossed at the ankles. Her light brown cowboy hat was resting on her belly, and she'd tilted her delicate chin up with her eyes closed, clearly savoring the warmth of the newly risen sun. Her red hair, loose and pulled over one shoulder, glinted like polished copper.

Peyton Halliday, in her worn boots, faded jeans, and white and baby-blue stripped light cotton western shirt was every cowboy's fantasy come to life.

And by every cowboy he meant him.

His mood automatically soured.

When she didn't open her eyes at his approach, he said, "I hope you have sunscreen on."

She pried one eye barely open and looked at him through a slit. "Of course, Dr. Drew."

He stopped at her feet, casting a shadow on her, and ran

a critical eye over her pale, lightly freckled skin trying to discern how long she'd been waiting for him. If she'd been sitting there long, she'd surely have a tint of red to her skin. Unless she really did have adequate sunscreen on.

He pinched his nose for a second and just asked, "How long have you been sitting here?"

She opened both eyes, able to look at him fully now because he was blocking the sun. "Not long. I figured you might be a little late into the clinic this morning."

Drew brought his teeth together. Had she seen him watching her trailer last night?

She smiled sweetly up at him. "With you having to be at the rodeo until the very end, and all."

She was messing with him. A muscle jumped beneath his eye. Fatigue. And stress. That was all. Nothing he hadn't successfully managed before to achieve his goals.

"You hungry?" she asked.

The way she asked it made him instantly think of all the different types of appetites a man could have, and he silently groaned.

For his sanity's sake, he shifted his gaze to the door she was leaning on and forced himself to think of the paperwork he was sure needed to be done on the other side of it. He'd planned on making up for his absence by doing the formal, electronic charting, if there was any first thing this morning. Doc tended to put off the chore because he didn't care for it. But Drew also knew Doc would have his hide if he put everyday mundane tasks ahead of doing what Doc had told him to do. Which was stick to Peyton like a bur.

He pulled in a lungful of crisp morning air and let it out slowly. "I could eat." He'd only chased all the coffee he'd drank with a single piece of toast, so yeah, he could definitely eat.

"Good, because I snagged this"—she put her hat on her head, sat up, and reached down to pick up from the ground a white paper bag he hadn't noticed before—"from the spread Nat always has brought in for the cast and crew. I'd feel guilty eating it all myself while we're on our way."

"On our way where?"

"To our next adventure." Her smile was dazzling even in the shade.

Growing still, he asked, "Which is?"

"Climbing Smith Rock."

Drew's jaw went slack. So much worse than zip-lining.

"I read all about it last night. While I was in my trailer." Her thick, long, burnished lashes swept down then back up as she gave him a slow, guileless blink.

Was this his payback for switching her mount last night? But she might not know for sure it was him who had arranged the switch. She could very well have seen him spying on her last night though.

At least he had a solid out for this adventure of hers. Unless she was also a practiced and accomplished rock climber as well as a competitive saddle bronc rider, there was no way she'd be able to even attempt scaling the dozens of routes up the many faces that made up the Smith Rock State Park.

He opened his mouth to say as much when she held up a finger to stop him.

"And by climb, I mean hike, of course. Turns out I left my climbing gear at home."

He snapped his mouth shut and raised his brows.

She laughed, and he felt the surprisingly husky sound behind his sternum. "No, I don't have climbing gear. And look at these arms." She stood on the bottom stair, making her as tall as his chin, and spread her arms wide. The white paper bag dangled from one hand and the buttons of her shirt strained between her breasts. "I'd never be able to reach the handholds, or whatever they're called." She dropped her arms with a shrug.

Drew probably should have said something, but his mind was suddenly completely blank. The rest of his body, however, had plenty to say. He did his damnedest to shut it down.

"But I would like to see the park. It looks beautiful in the pictures on the internet." She blinked up at him in a more genuine way, her gaze skipping over his face.

He realized he was hot. Very hot.

"So, will you?"

Why yes, yes, I will. "Will I what?"

She laughed again. "Drive me to Smith Rock? If you can't, no worries. I can get an Uber since my truck is in the shop. But either way, I need to get out of here before Nat finds me."

Knowing what Doc would tell him to do, Drew nodded. "Sure. I will drive you to Smith Rock. Today would be a perfect day for a scenic walk."

"Hike." She corrected him. "A scenic hike."

He gestured toward their feet. "In cowboy boots?"

"If you can't do it in boots, it ain't worth doin', son." She winked at him.

It took an extreme force of will for Drew not to graphically imagine one thing in particular that could be done with boots on. Nothing but boots...

He cleared his throat. "Okay, then. Hike." A nice scenic, and safe, hike. One that lasted long enough to make her miss her ride this evening.

Suddenly, Drew wasn't feeling quite so exhausted, after all.

PEYTON HAD TO give it to Drew. He was hard to ruffle.

But the day was young.

She had a definite spring in her step as she went to wait for Drew at his truck. She'd passed on his invitation to go into the sports medicine trailer with him while he grabbed them bottled water to take with them on their "hike." The last place she would ever willingly go was a medical clinic. Even when the medical professional looked like Drew Neisson.

She didn't have to wait long before Drew rounded the end of the trailer with a drawstring topped, black nylon knapsack in one hand. Far more practical for a hike than her pastry-filled white paper bag. He hit a button on his key fob, and the truck doors unlocked with a *thunk*.

Peyton wasted no time climbing in the passenger side. She assumed Nat and the crew were still eating breakfast in the *Buckin' TV* RV, but on the off chance someone came looking for her, she wanted to be able to duck out of sight. According to the Smith Rock Park's website, the rock formation and its trails were considerably closer to them than Mt. Bachelor, so she wasn't concerned about being back to the rodeo grounds in time for the women's exhibition rides.

And as annoyed as she was about her father's attempt to control her from afar by arranging for Drew, a doctor, to shadow her, as she watched him climb into the big truck, all long muscular legs and broad shoulders, she had to admit things could be worse.

Drew carefully maneuvered his truck out of the increasingly busy rodeo grounds and headed for the highway, turning in the opposite direction they'd taken yesterday when they'd gone to Mt. Bachelor. The farther they traveled, the more opposite the landscape became, also. Instead of driving toward lodge pole and ponderosa pine-covered foothills, they were surrounded by the scrub brush-covered epitome of high desert, broken up by the verdant green of irrigated fields.

In the distance, their destination was clear. Jutting up from the flatness were incredible, distinct spires of seemingly sheer rock, with craggy, uneven tops.

Peyton sat forward in her seat with a gasp. "It's beautiful." Then she twisted to see out of the truck's windows behind them, and her heart soared.

DREW KNEW THE view that would greet her was a string of stunning, snow-tipped mountains of the central Cascades.

"You are so lucky. Everything is so beautiful here."

Drew grinned. "I wouldn't trade it."

She faced forward, her growing excitement palpable. Her beautiful profile practically glowed with happy anticipation. She definitely was an adrenaline junkie. Little wonder she willingly climbed aboard broncs.

"Did you always want to be a bronc rider?"

She laughed. "I didn't even know it was an option until I saw the other girls competing on their circuit in Texas last year."

"You've only been riding saddle broncs for a year?"

"More like three months."

He shot her a glance. "What? You've only been riding for three months?"

"No, I've been riding since before I could walk. I've been ranch saddle bronc riding for three months."

"But you successfully rode Karen From Finance." He couldn't keep the incredulity from his voice. Because he was absolutely incredulous.

"Right?" She grinned impishly. "My grandpa's ranch manager always says there isn't a horse alive that can make me eat mud."

"You've never been thrown?"

"Well, I've definitely fallen off. Tends to happen when you do something wrong."

"Sometimes, it also just happens. I know as much from personal experience."

She shrugged in a *it sucks to suck* way.

Drew bit back a smile and returned his attention to the road. Despite her bravado, Peyton's inexperience might also explain her family's insistence she be watched over. "How does your family feel about you riding broncs?"

She gave him a look that made clear what she thought of his deduction abilities. "I know you already know how they feel."

"Regardless of your natural abilities, you can't blame them for being concerned about you doing something so inherently dangerous."

She muttered, "But I can blame them for being smothering."

Drew's curiosity was instantly piqued. "Why are they smothering?"

"Did you always want to be a doctor?" she not-so-smoothly changed the subject.

He readjusted his hands on the wheel. "I did."

He could feel her gaze on him, probably waiting for him to say more. He wasn't going to, so she'd just have to wait.

He heard her huff out a breath. "Okay, so while all the other little boys were out playing cowboy, you were busy playing doctor."

He snorted. "In a way." But certainly not in the way she was implying. Mostly, he'd made himself invisible while the real doctors worked.

She fell silent, apparently satisfied.

As they approached the park, Peyton strained forward in her seat again, letting out little gasps as each new feature of the rock formations was revealed, some shadowed, some bathed in the warm morning light.

She reached out and grabbed his shoulder. "Thank you so much for bringing me here. I have never in my life seen so many shades of red and brown. And I'm from Texas."

Her small hand was not surprisingly strong and warm. He had to think hard to focus. The gradient of rock did vary in color from level to level, a function of time, erosion, and different types of rock making up the spine formations.

She gave his arm a small squeeze before slipping it away.

Drew started to turn toward the yurt Welcome Center, but Peyton waved him forward. "I read about a bridge we need to cross and that there's parking reasonably close by. Can we just go to the bridge?"

"Sure. Yeah, sure." While he would have preferred wasting as much time as possible in the complete safety of the visitor's center, he knew there were several very flat, very tame trails along the Crooked River that wound around the rocks. "We just need to grab a parking pass first." He pulled into one of the fee stations, hopped out, and bought a park day pass from one of the automated fee station kiosks.

The park was a popular place no matter the time of year, but they were lucky and found an open parking space as close as they could get to the foot bridge that crossed the meandering river. Drew put the white paper bag Peyton had brought into the knapsack before they climbed from the truck.

Slinging the knapsack over his shoulder, Drew led Peyton down the steep, semi-paved walkway, past the resting spots and the large grassy area with picnic tables and a bathroom. He let her go first over the foot bridge that spanned the crystal clear, relatively shallow and aptly named Crooked River. Her excitement was as contagious as it had been the day before when they'd zip-lined, and as before, he found himself smiling. Peyton's enjoyment of pretty much everything was infectious.

Clinical, not personal.

When she reached the end of the bridge, and the lightly graveled path split into three separate trails, Drew called, "Go left."

Peyton stopped to read the trail marker. "Wolf Tree Trail?"

"Yep," Drew confirmed as he reached her. A very scenic, very tame hike right along the river.

"I was hoping to check out Misery Ridge."

Drew laughed. "Of course, you were."

She contemplated the trail for a moment, then shrugged. "Okay. Come on." She snagged his hand and pulled him forward.

Drew found himself being pulled along both physically and emotionally. What was it about this woman? Before he knew it, he was threading his fingers between hers.

She glanced up at him, as if surprised, but then smiled.

He felt it right in his gut. Damn, she was pretty.

She asked, "So, you come here often?" then laughed at the unintentional pick-up sounding line.

A woman like her would never have to use any sort of line to get a guy to talk to her.

His fingers flexed on her hand of their own volition, then he turned his attention to the beautiful scenery. Vibrant green native grass interspersed with wild flowers grew on both sides of the trail, especially thick and lush on the banks of the river. "Not often enough."

"A case of not appreciating what's in your own back-yard?"

"Exactly." It would have been easy to blame it on school, or his chosen career, but she was right. There was so much in his life he hadn't fully appreciated.

Like having the chance to take a hike with a pretty girl.

She looked up at the face of Picnic Lunch Wall and a set of climbers already making their way up the set lines. "I'd be here constantly."

He'd consider it with company like her.

When the trail narrowed, and there was no longer room for them to walk side-by-side, he was forced to release her hand. Which finally brought him to his senses. This was not a date.

The trail led them beneath a giant ponderosa tree, and Peyton gasped at the sight of a strategically placed bench at the tree's base, well within its shade but still offering a stunning view of the river.

"Now that's a perfect place to eat breakfast," Peyton exclaimed and hurried to the bench. Grinning wide, she plopped onto the seat and patted the spot next to her.

And Drew's senses deserted him yet again.

Before taking the seat he very much wanted to occupy, with his leg pressed against hers, their shoulders touching, he slid the knapsack off his shoulder. She reached out and took it from him. As he sat, she pulled open the drawstring top and took out the bag and the waters, handing him one.

She opened the bag. "Giant blueberry cake masquerading as a muffin or an equally giant apple fritter?"

"Mm, nutritious. You go ahead and choose what you want."

"There's two of each. Go for it." She held the open bag to him.

He fished out a sticky apple fritter that was indeed huge.

"Good choice. They're my favorite." She pulled the other fritter from the bag for herself.

"No wonder you have so much energy."

She winked and took a big bite.

They sat in companionable silence eating their sticky pastries, drinking their waters, and enjoying the view.

But in his head, he kept hearing her muttered response and wanted to know more. "Why does your family smother you?"

She kept her gaze upriver, chewing slowly. She shrugged and swallowed. "Baby of the family."

He thought of Alec, the baby of their family, and wondered if he had become a bull rider because he'd felt smothered. Drew immediately rejected the idea. Alec had become a bull rider because of their mom. The same reason Drew had gone into medicine.

Peyton popped the last of her fitter into her mouth. "Do you want more?" At his head shake, she rolled the top of the bag closed and returned it and her half-empty water bottle to the knapsack.

Drew took it from her, put his water bottle in also, and slung it over his shoulder again as he stood. He had to turn away when she started to suck the sticky frosting off her fingers.

Peyton popped up off the bench. "And there's the sugar rush! Okay, let's keep going."

Since his ultimate goal was to keep her away from the rodeo grounds for as long as possible, Drew touched a finger to the brim of his hat. "Yes, ma'am."

They walked a little farther, with Peyton snapping pictures on her phone. When she stopped in front of a large boulder at least fifteen feet tall with about a one-inch crack running down its face, standing apart from the rest of the formation, Drew assumed she was simply going to take another photo.

Instead, she tucked her phone into her jeans pocket and announced, "This one's perfect."

"Perfect for what?"

She spread her hands wide. "Bouldering!" She sent him what he was beginning to think of as her *here comes trouble* smile. "You don't need climbing equipment for bouldering."

"You're wearing cowboy boots."

"I thought we already established I do everything in cowboy boots."

Luckily, she turned back toward the boulder before she could see him gulp.

"And I have you to catch me if I fall."

Drew stilled. That was what he was here for, wasn't it?

But there was something about the way she said the words that made his chest ache. He didn't have time to analyze the feeling because Peyton was already scrambling her way up the boulder, wedging her fingers and the toes of her boots into the crack in the rock.

Setting the knapsack on the ground, he hurried to stand directly below her in case he did need to catch her. But Peyton made it to the top of the boulder without a single slip.

She stood and faced him, thrusting her fists over her head in victory. "Woohoo! Bouldering. Check." She made a giant checkmark in the air.

Drew found himself laughing, sucked into her joy again. He put his hands on his hips. "Congratulations. Now, how are you going to get down?"

She dropped her hands and looked around as if she hadn't considered the problem.

Drew took pity on her. He stepped closer and raised his hands. "Sit down and slide. I'll catch you."

"And I'll scrape all the flesh from by backside."

"Lucky for you, I'm a doctor."

She sobered. "Yeah, I know."

He encouraged her with a wiggle of his fingers. But after she sat and started scooching down the slightly curved rock, he said, "Push yourself off, away from the rock, and I'll catch you."

Her warm hazel eyes locked with his.

Was she gauging if she could trust him?

Drew wasn't able to consider the question more because

she pushed herself from the boulder and extended her arms toward him. He caught her easily, his hands on her waist and hers on his shoulders.

And her gaze never left his.

He slid her down his body until her booted feet were on the ground. Her breasts were warm on his chest.

He'd never wanted to kiss a woman more in his life.

But she blinked, patted him on the chest, and stepped away enough that he had to release her. "We better get back to the rodeo grounds, Dr. Drew. You have cowboys to patch up, and I have broncs to bust." She snagged his knapsack and headed back down the trail.

Drew tipped his head back and stared up at the clear blue sky. He might as well get *I am so screwed* tattooed on him somewhere.

CHAPTER ELEVEN

I N DREW'S TRUCK on their way back from Smith Rock State Park, despite her best efforts, Peyton couldn't stop thinking about the look in Drew Neisson's light blue eyes. Let alone the feel of his hot, muscular body as she'd slid down it, feeling every hard inch of him.

Her plan had been to get his heart pounding, but hers still beat like a farrier's hammer in her chest.

The walk back to his truck had been a blur, her awareness firmly focused on the man shadowing her. And once inside his truck, with him seated so close, close enough to touch, she found her throat too tight to speak and her palms damp.

She expected him to try to delay her return to the rodeo grounds, but he drove them straight back with hardly a word. Did he regret the way he'd looked at her? Like he'd wanted to kiss her more than he wanted his next breath?

Or had he correctly guessed that she would have let him?

Maybe it was worse still, that he considered her a patient, of sorts, and she'd made him uncomfortable with her lame flirtation?

Her face heated with the possibility.

Drew pulled into his space next to the sports medicine clinic trailer and turned to look at her. Ready to bolt, Peyton released her seat belt and grabbed the door handle.

Drew's deep voice stopped her. "It's my turn to thank you for today. I had fun. Plus, I'd forgotten how beautiful Smith Rock is. Thank you for suggesting we go there."

At least part of her embarrassment left her in a cooling rush. He didn't regret spending the day with her. Which maybe meant he didn't consider her his patient. She smiled. "You're welcome. Thank you for taking me. And for catching me."

The same intensity darkened his eyes again. "You're welcome. That's why I'm here."

The reminder that he had been tasked with keeping her safe definitely ruined the mood. Whatever that mood was, exactly.

She gave him a curt nod and hopped out of his truck.

"Peyton," he called after her.

She paused in the act of shutting the passenger door. "Yeah?"

"I'll see you later."

Not if I see you first. "Okay." She swung the door shut and hurried on her way.

Maybe it was time for her to focus on fulfilling her contract with *Buckin' TV*. The best way to do that would be find the girls and see if anyone would be willing to trade their rides with her for this evening. She didn't trust the Neisson boys not to switch one of their duds again for the bronc she'd drawn out of the hat this morning before she'd snagged muffins and fritters. With the ladies' rides for exhibition purposes only, which bronc they rode really didn't matter. Except to the ladies themselves. As she'd told Drew, they were competitors, after all. But fortunately for Peyton, not all the girls liked an over-the-top wild bucking ride and were willing to trade.

She was heading toward the large RV Nat had rented for the crew when she thought she heard her name being called.

"Peyton! Over here!" Sammie beckoned her from where the women and the crew were congregated near the pens that held rough stock before they were funneled into the arena.

Peyton changed direction and hurried over to Sammie and the other girls.

Climbing up onto the pen fencing next to Sammie and hooking her arms over the top rail, she asked, "What's going on?"

"Generating content, baby." Sammie shoulder-bumped her and pointed into the pen, currently filled with very big, very wooly sheep that were used in place of anything larger and more dangerous for the kids to ride during the junior portion of the rodeo. Beth was climbing down into the pen while Nat had the guys filming and recording her.

Still confused, Peyton asked, "What is she doing?"

"She's going to try to ride a sheep."

Peyton laughed. "No way. She's too tall." Beth was almost as tall as Sammie.

"Doesn't mean she isn't going to try."

Sure enough, Beth grabbed tufts of wool of the nearest sheep and swung her leg over the poor thing's back. Peyton shouldn't have felt sorry for the sheep because it took all of two seconds to send Beth flying with a leap and buck that would make any bronc proud.

The other women hanging on the fence whooped and clapped as Beth stood, brushing off her backside and signaling she was unhurt.

Knowing she was far better suited for riding a sheep, Peyton said, "I'm getting in on that action."

"Yes! Go, girl!" Sammie cheered her on as Peyton climbed through the pen fencing and started working her way toward the clustered sheep slowly so as not to spook them any more than they already were. Her grandfather didn't raise sheep on the family ranch, but rough stock was rough stock as far as Peyton was concerned. She just needed to keep her approach slow and calm.

"Easy, babies," she cooed as she eased her way toward a likely subject. The sheep watched her with what she assumed was suspicion with its big, wet, dark eyes. "That's right. Don't worry about little ol' me. I'm just gonna take a quick sit down on one of you sweeties."

Peyton sidled up to the sheep she'd chosen, pausing for a moment to reassure the animal. The tactic seemed to work because the sheep turned its head away from her. Seizing the opportunity, Peyton grabbed handfuls of wool near the sheep's shoulders and swung a leg over its back just as the animal bolted into motion. Instead of leaping and bucking as the sheep Beth had tried to ride had done, this sheep just broke into a run around the perimeter of the pen.

Peyton stayed as low as she could and gripped with her

legs, but even as short as they were, they still dragged on the ground. The resistance didn't slow the sheep any, and when it veered close to the fence, her shoulder hit violently enough to knock her off. She landed hard on her back, but the pain blazing through her shoulder and down her arm eclipsed everything else. She grabbed at the point of impact with her free hand.

Though she was pretty sure she was lying in sheep shit, she needed a minute to breathe her way through the pain. Something she'd become very good at as a kid.

Though her eyes were squeezed shut, she sensed something looming over her. God help her if it was the back end of a sheep.

"Peyton. Peyton, look at me." It was Drew. Using what she guessed to be his doctor voice.

Great. She opened one eye. Drew was on one knee in the sheep doo next to her, his hat pushed high on his forehead. Dang, he was cute.

He grazed his fingertips along her temples. "Did you hit your head as well as your shoulder?"

She released her injured shoulder and slid her hand onto her chest. The last thing she needed was him calling her dad and telling him she was hurt. "I didn't hit my shoulder. Or my head." At least half of that was true. To try to prove she was in better condition than she felt, she sat up and had to bite back a groan.

"I saw that sheep try to scrape you off on the fence. I know you hit your shoulder. At the very least." He reached across her and gently touched her shoulder, probing the joint. She pressed her lips tight to keep from hissing.

"Can you move that arm?"

Though it sent a blaze of pain through her, she lifted her arm and rotated it fully as much for herself as for Drew. Thankfully, she had full range of motion.

Nat leaned down next to them. "Is she hurt?"

Peyton said, "No."

At the same time, Drew said, "I don't think so."

Peyton shot him a glance. She'd totally expected him to say that she was injured. At least enough to keep her from riding later.

Nat straightened. "Excellent. We got some great footage. You just made up for being M.I.A. for the majority of today and yesterday, Peyton." She turned and picked her way back out of the sheep pen, her arms held high as if manure could levitate.

Drew rose up off his knee and offered Peyton a hand.

She slipped her hand into his, the connection instantly familiar. Holding his hand as they'd walked along the trail, their fingers intertwined, had been...nice. This time, as he wrapped his big, warm hand around hers and hoisted her carefully out of the poop, that nice feeling changed to very, very nice. Especially when he was reacting so calmly to her hurting herself riding a sheep, of all things.

He retained her hand after she was on her feet, but once again tested her other arm and shoulder with his free hand. "I think you probably just got a stinger."

"A stinger?"

"Basically, an angry nerve. The pain should fade. Especially after being iced."

Fading would be good. She really wanted the fading part, and soon.

His gaze shifted to something behind them, and she turned to see Natalie motioning for her crew to enter the pen and move closer to Peyton and Drew. He released her hand, but not abruptly. He trailed his fingers along hers in a way that made her completely forget about her shoulder. And the fact that he was a doctor.

Stepping away from her, Drew bent and picked up her hat that had been knocked from her head when she landed.

Maybe she *had* hit her head. Which would explain the warm fuzzies Drew was stirring in her.

Brushing dirt and other unpleasantness from her hat, he handed it to her, then stepped close enough to run his hands over her head. Her brain recognized that he was examining her for any bumps or tender spots, clearly not willing to take her word for having not hit her head. Her body, on the other hand, processed his touch as a very pleasurable, if not downright erotic, caress. Despite her best efforts, she found herself closing her eyes and tilting her head back as she soaked up the sensations.

His hands dropped away, and she opened her eyes to find him stepping back and adjusting his own hat on his head. He checked the progress of Nat, Dan, and Phil, who were struggling to get the big camera either through or over the pen fencing, then looked back at her. "You know, my siblings and I used to ride these fluffy demons every chance we got at the junior rodeo. Crazy, but a ton of fun."

Bemused, Peyton smiled at him. Now she had her explanation as to why he wasn't spitting mad at her. Which would undoubtedly change if he knew how badly her shoulder was hurting her at the moment. She'd been around rodeo and ranching enough to know if she'd done serious damage to her shoulder or arm, like dislocation, separation, or a break, there would be no way she could move it as much as she could. So, she didn't feel stupid for hiding the throbbing agony. And blessedly, it was her non-dominate hand. She'd be good to ride tonight. She hoped.

She started to return her hat to her head when Drew stopped her.

"Uhm, you have…*sheep* in your hair."

"Which you were just touching!" She shuddered.

"Which is why I know it's there."

"Eww." She shuddered again and turned toward the pen fence. "I'm going to take a shower. And you need to wash your hands!"

She heard him laughing behind her. "Good idea on both counts."

Nat yelled, "Hey, where are you going? I want to get footage of him examining you."

The memory of Drew's fingers in her hair and the very sexual response she'd had to it made Peyton's face flame with embarrassment. Without turning, she responded, "I have sheep shit in my hair. I'm going to shower." With a wave, she climbed through the pen fencing to the cheers of her fellow Buckin' Babes.

And the minute she was done showering, or maybe before, she was going to ice her shoulder so Drew wouldn't know that she was pretty sure she hadn't just given herself *a stinger* and risk him calling her family.

DREW PULLED IN a decidedly sheep-scented breath and tried to return his pulse to normal. The feminine shouts had redirected him from heading to the arena where he'd intended on looking for his boss to ask again if there was any way he could find someone else to play nanny to their benefactor's wild child. Because Drew had almost kissed her. A fact he'd keep to himself for so, so many reasons, but couldn't be ignored.

His gut had told him if he didn't go see what the women he'd correctly suspected to be a part of the exhibition bronc riding group were up to, he'd regret it.

And he'd been right.

He'd barely approached the pen holding sheep to be used for the junior rodeo later in the day when he heard shouts of *go, Peyton*, and *ride it like you stole it*. He didn't have to have firsthand knowledge of rodeo shenanigans to figure out what Peyton's fellow riders were cheering her to do.

He'd broke into a run and reached the pen fencing in time to see Peyton snag and mount a sheep, which in turn took her for a wild ride around the edge of the pen. As a kid, he'd clung to similar sheep in mad dashes across the arena, only to end up sprawled in the dirt as adults cheered raucously from the stands.

Peyton at first appeared to be faring better than most kids, the natural riding abilities she'd claimed to possess in obvious display. But then the sheep had veered toward the pen fencing, either out of panic or in an attempt to scrap her off, and she'd hit a glancing blow to her shoulder on a metal fence post. The impact had reverberated through the tube railing he'd been gripping as he watched. It had to have hurt and had knocked her off the sheep's back.

Drew had had the same exact thing happen to him when he'd been about ten. Only he'd been on the back of one of his grandfather's yearling bulls that he'd been dared to ride by Liam. The young bull had definitely tried to scrap him off its back by hitting the paddock fence as it ran. Drew's arm had gone momentarily numb from the blow, resulting in what his oldest brother Ian had called a stinger. It sucked for a hot minute, but then went away without any real damage or lasting effect.

After seeing the same thing happen to Peyton, Drew's heart had remained in his throat, though, until Peyton moved her shoulder in a full circle, and he'd reassured himself that her head hadn't bounced off the ground when she fell.

He'd been disturbingly loathed to release her hand once he had a hold of it. He'd been assigned to keep her safe, but after only a few days in her presence, he found himself wanting to keep her safe in more ways than just from injury.

It seemed he was failing, miserably, at his attempt to keep things clinical, not personal.

PEYTON GROANED LONG and loud as she settled into the bed in her little trailer, holding an ice pack against her upper arm and shoulder. She'd hoped a couple of over-the-counter anti-inflammatories and a hot shower would ease the throbbing pain from where she'd hit the pen fencing, but they hadn't. At least not enough. And when Sammie and Nat had checked on her not long after she'd emerged from the shower and found Peyton free of sheep poo but still in pain, Nat had declared that Peyton could take the night off from the ladies' exhibition ride. She'd earned it by providing great content with her mostly successful sheep ride.

Peyton still hadn't decided how she felt about missing her chance to ride. While she hated to let anything, especially a physical ailment, get the better of her, she also didn't want to get bucked off a bronc because she wasn't at her best. But what Dr. Drew had declared a stinger was turning out to be a nasty lump despite constant icing and was already turning all sorts of interesting colors. She continued to be able to move it, though, which gave her hope.

Dressed in light flannel, gray and blue checked lounge pants and a dark blue cotton T-shirt, she tried to get as comfortable as she could propped up by pillows in bed. She settled her computer on her lap with the intention of watching a movie, but the roar of the crowd attending the night's rodeo kept distracting her. If only she could make out what the announcer was saying over the PA. She'd be able to close her eyes and envision the action, thus not feel as though she was missing out.

But she couldn't discern what the announcer was saying. She couldn't envision what was happening and thus feel a part of the action. She felt the sharp bite of missed opportunities.

She didn't fear missing out. She hated it.

Lurching up on her bed, she yanked the curtains of the small window over the bed closed and turned the volume on her computer up.

It didn't help.

Maybe she should just get dressed and go to the arena. If the girls were still riding, she could at least help. And if they were done, then she could make Nat happy by hanging on the fence with the rest of the ladies oohing and ahhing over the guys competing in the main rodeo.

But would she be able to be right there, at the chutes, and not take her opportunity to ride? Probably not. And if she was thrown because she wasn't operating at one hundred percent, then wouldn't she be validating her family's concerns? Absolutely. She couldn't prove their point that she wasn't physically up to experiencing life the way she wanted to by being dumb. Far better to miss one night of competing than miss everything.

Peyton resettled the ice pack on her shoulder and her computer on her lap, then scrolled through her downloads for another movie to watch.

A firm knock sounded on the trailer door.

Assuming it was Sammie or Nat checking on her again, Peyton set the ice pack and computer aside and padded barefoot to the door. She turned the lock and opened the door.

And found Drew standing nearly eye to eye with her, his white hat held in his hands and unquestionable concern darkening his blue eyes. His dark blond hair looked like his fingers had been pulled through it more than once.

"Drew," she said inanely.

"You weren't at the chutes for your ride," he answered just as inanely.

Obviously, she wasn't at the chutes because she was standing in her trailer wearing pajamas. "Did you and your brother have another *deadly* mount picked out for me? As in, silent but deadly?"

His gaze dropped to his boots, and he worried his hat brim between his hands. *Busted.*

He blew out a breath and lifted his eyes to her. "Are you okay?"

She shifted, turning her bruised and swollen arm away from him. "Of course. I'm fine."

His gaze flicked from her high ponytail to her bare feet. Assessing.

He was a doctor, but she still found herself wishing she'd pulled on a sweatshirt over her thin T-shirt. There was something about the way he looked at her that made her respond in all sorts of embarrassingly obvious ways. And while he might be her babysitter, he wasn't her doctor.

Drew took a step forward. "Can I come in?"

"Why?"

"I need to make sure you're okay."

"You're not my doctor, Drew." She had to say the words. To remind them both.

"But I *am* a doctor. Contracted by the rodeo and hired by your—"

"All right, all right." She huffed and moved away from the door so he could enter her trailer.

She plopped down on the bench and pulled her sleeve up so he could easily see where she'd hit the fence pole.

Drew stepped inside and closed the door behind him with a soft click. Placing his hat down on the dinette table, he sat down next to her. Only a slight frown betrayed his concern as he ran gentle fingers over the bruised lump on her upper arm.

"That's quite a hematoma you have brewing. Do you have pain?"

Uh, yeah.

She lied, "Not much. It looks a lot worse than it is."

A blond eyebrow twitched up.

She smiled to sell the lie.

He touched the bruised area again, his fingers feather-light. "Your skin is cold. You icing?"

Her breath caught in her throat, and she would have sworn her skin was on fire, instead of being cold. "Yes."

He nodded. "Good." He lifted her arm again, raising his gaze to hers as if watching for pain.

"Drew?"

"Yeah?"

"You're not my doctor, right?" She couldn't help how breathless she sounded.

He didn't answer for what seemed forever, then finally said, "Not if you don't want me to be."

Her gaze dropped to his mouth of its own volition. "No offense, but I'd rather you weren't."

His lips parted in a sensuous smile. "No offense taken, Peyton."

Then he kissed her.

CHAPTER TWELVE

THE SECOND DREW'S mouth connected with Peyton's, all thoughts of how badly his attempts at keeping her from harm were going evaporated from his brain. All he could think of was how much he wanted her.

The first touch of his lips to hers had been tentative, needing to make sure he hadn't misread the hunger in her gaze. But when she opened to him and swayed toward him, he reached for the back of her head and deepened the kiss. She tasted as good as she smelled. Better. Like honey.

One of her small, strong hands gripped his shirt, and the other skimmed his jaw, holding his face as he was holding her head. Their tongues met with an electric jolt that exploded through him.

Peyton moaned as if feeling the effects of the kiss as much as he was. She kissed the same way she did everything, with a zest and joy that pulled him to her.

Wanting to pull her to him in actuality, he reached for her shoulder. Peyton instantly shied away, breaking off their kiss with a sharp inhale.

Realization hit him like a cold dunk in a water trough. He'd grabbed hold of her injured arm. He released her and pulled back.

"Shit, Peyton, I'm so sorry."

"It's okay. Really. I guess we both got a little carried away."

Was she regretting the kiss? Drew ran a hand over his face and tried to get a grip on the desire she'd unleashed in him. What had he been thinking? "No, really. I'm sorry. You're hurt. Which is why I knocked on your door in the first place."

One side of her delectable mouth kicked up. "Instead of just lurking outside?"

"I'm sorry about that, too, but—"

"Drew, it's okay. You don't have to keep apologizing. I'm sure my dad is paying you a lot to keep me—"

"Whoa, hang on." Anger, instant and hot, swept through him. "I am not being paid by your father to—" He stopped himself just as abruptly as he'd stopped her.

Technically, her father, or at least her family's business, was indeed paying him. As long as the Hallidays were going to provide money to run the sports medicine clinic, they were his bosses. He was crossing so many lines just by being here with her, let alone wanting her. Not to mention the lines he'd drawn for himself to keep his heart safe. It was Peyton's nature to put herself at risk. No way could he fall for someone he might lose like he'd lost his mother.

He quickly stood and took a step back from her. He kept his gaze fastened on her bruised and swollen arm to keep from being derailed again by her sweet mouth or warm gaze. "I better get back to the arena." Even though Drew knew full well that Doc didn't want him there as long as Peyton was here. But with her in pajamas and tending to her injury, Drew was confident she wouldn't get up to any more trouble. "Keep icing that arm, and if it isn't better in the morning, come by the clinic, and we'll take a closer look at it."

"I will. Thanks," she said flatly. She didn't move, just sat watching him as he picked up his hat and moved to the door.

He hesitated with his hand on the latch, wanting to say more, feeling as though he should, but having no idea what to say. It was a simple fact that he just didn't have enough experience dealing with kissing women he shouldn't have kissed. Burying himself in his studies had always been the simpler, safer choice.

Peyton said, "Thanks for coming to check on me. But don't worry, I'm fine." She sounded as though she'd said those exact same words a thousand times.

Drew glanced back at her, finally meeting her hazel gaze. She revealed nothing.

With a curt nod, he opened the trailer door and left, the taste of her still on his lips.

THE SECOND THE trailer door *snicked* closed behind Drew, Peyton slumped back against the padded bench seat. Why had she kissed Dr. Andrew Neisson? Or had he kissed her? She couldn't remember.

And who, exactly, had initiated the kiss didn't really matter, considering they had both kissed each other back. Peyton's skin, as well as other things, were still tingling from the feel of Drew's lips on hers.

She pushed herself up off the bench and went to her bed. Flopping down, she grabbed up the ice pack she'd set aside when Drew had knocked on the door. But instead of putting the pack back on her shoulder, she settled it on her forehead. When that didn't cool her down, she put it against her upper chest.

What had she been thinking? It was one thing to mess with one of her father's lackies, especially the ones tasked with keeping her on the kind of short leash he preferred. She knew her dad did it out of love, but the older she became the harder it was to tolerate.

But what had just happened with Drew had been stupid. She'd known that she was attracted to him, so she should have never let him into the trailer. Who would have guessed such a cold fish, as Sammie had called him, would turn out to be so hot?

And who would have guessed how much she was starting to like him?

Drew had intended to go straight from Peyton's trailer to the arena, but he needed to walk off the lust coursing through his veins first, so he'd wandered around the rows of competitors and stock contractors' RVs, trailers, and campers.

Keep one bronc rider safe, that was all he had to do to ensure the security of the sports medicine clinic. To ensure his future.

Having fun with her, holding her hand, sliding her down his body when all he'd needed to do was set her on the ground, kissing her... He rubbed the back of his neck. He could lose everything he'd worked for all these years with such foolishness.

He needed to find a different way to fulfill his so-called assignment. He tilted his head back as if inspiration might come from the star-studded night sky. It didn't. No huge surprise. He blew out a breath and looked around him, noticing for the first time that his wandering had taken him down the row where the large *Buckin' TV* RV was parked. There were a lot of lights on inside, and he could hear what sounded like a television. Though the rodeo was still going, the women's exhibition rides were over. It wasn't surprising that the crew had returned to their RV.

An idea actually did occur to him, though he seriously doubted it was heaven sent. Mostly because he intended to lie. He would tell Natalie that he planned to use his authority through sports medicine to pull Peyton from the exhibition because of the injury to her arm.

Drew strode to the RV's door and knocked before he changed his mind. The sound man opened the door, raising his brows at Drew.

"Is Natalie available?" Drew asked.

"Who are you?" The guy apparently didn't recognize

Drew in the poor light.

"Dr. Drew Neisson." He threw in the *doctor* so he wouldn't be mistaken for some reality television wannabe. Though frankly he couldn't imagine there were many here in the Pineville rodeo community.

Natalie called from within the recreational vehicle, "Is that Peyton's babysitter, Phil?"

This time the sound guy—Phil—lifted a single questioning brow at Drew.

"It is," Drew answered.

Phil leaned back and yelled to Natalie, "Yep."

"Get him in here," Natalie responded.

Drew was ushered into the plush RV where nearly every horizontal space was occupied by some sort of video recording or editing equipment. Natalie and the cameraman were seated at the dinette table staring at a monitor.

Without looking up, the executive producer waved him to her. "Perfect timing. Come here and sit down. We're just putting together an extended segment on Miss Halliday. And I need you to sign this waiver." She slid a piece of paper along the table in front of an unoccupied spot on the U-shaped dinette bench. Then she slapped a pen on top of it.

Drew sat down and moved the pen aside. "A waiver for what?"

"For us to use your image and name on the show."

Drew set the pen back on top of the paper and pushed them both away from him. "No thanks." He seriously doubted Peyton's family would appreciate him using the assignment they'd given him, through Doc, for a chance to be on television. Nor would his own grandfather.

She shot him a perturbed look, then returned her attention to the monitor. "Maybe you'll change your mind after you see this." She turned the monitor so he could see it. To the cameraman she said, "Wind it back to the beginning of the segment and turn up the sound."

On the screen appeared a still shot of a smiling Peyton standing in an arena with hands in the air in clear jubilation, obviously celebrating a successful bronc ride and looking incredibly beautiful. The image morphed into a photo of Peyton as a child—an adorable, radiant, definitely joyful kid—and a voice-over by Natalie telling the story of Peyton Halliday, youngest grandchild of billionaire Harold Halliday.

A doted upon golden child, Peyton's life had almost taken a tragic turn at the age of ten when she had to undergo open-heart surgery. But because she is a fighter, Peyton overcame her childhood illness and went on to be a daredevil of the first order. The screen was then filled with images of Peyton riding a dirt bike, climbing out of a race car, and dangling from a hang-glider. The piece ended with the footage of Peyton's ride on the sheep, including her hitting the pen fencing with a teeth-rattling force, then Drew leaning over her with his hand on her shoulder.

Drew realized he had gotten off easy in regard to the extracurricular activities Peyton had wanted to try while here in Pineville. More importantly, he now had a better understanding for why her family had been willing to pay out a huge chunk of cash in exchange for her safety.

When the piece ended, Natalie asked, "What do you

think?"

"Why did she have to have the surgery?" Drew asked instead of giving his opinion of the blatantly salacious segment. They were definitely going for the poor-little-rich-girl angle.

Natalie said, "I was hoping you could tell me. I don't think it's a coincidence that you, a medical professional, were hired to keep an eye on her."

Neither did Drew. But as a medical professional, he wasn't about to even speculate about Peyton's health, either current or past. "I'm obviously bound by HIPAA. Didn't she have to sign a medical release form when she auditioned to join the exhibition tour?"

"She did. One that allows us to reveal any medical issues of note. Which is how we learned about the open-heart surgery. And to be frank, it was why we picked her to be on the show out of the dozens of applicants."

The cameraman muttered, "Though her being a billionaire oil tycoon's granddaughter would have been enough to get her chosen."

Nat waved him off in a *yeah-yeah* way. "I mean, who rides broncs after going through something like open-heart surgery?"

Someone who wants to really live, Drew thought.

Nat shook her head, not with concern, but with pure reality TV glee.

No wonder Peyton was forever trying to ditch the television producer. To Natalie, Peyton was just something to exploit. Drew found himself growing angry. It was time to go.

Straight back to Peyton to get some very important questions answered.

PEYTON WAS HITTING the rewind button for the second time on the sci-fi movie she was trying to watch, but her mind kept wandering to the lips of a certain cowboy when a forceful knock on her trailer door made her jump. Since Drew had said he was returning to the arena, Sammie, or maybe some of the other girls, must be coming to check on her.

A warmth born of unexpected friendship filled Peyton despite the ice pack balanced on her shoulder and upper arm. She'd join the *Buckin' TV* cast for adventure but had found so much more.

"Come on in," she hollered, knowing she hadn't locked the door after Drew had left. If only she had made popcorn. But her mind had been firmly stuck on a different sort of snack thanks to Drew Neisson.

She heard the door click open, but instead of Sammie or Beth or any of the other girls flitting into the trailer, all hair and chatter, the man who had been dominating her thoughts stepped inside and instantly made the space smaller.

She just stared at him. Had he come to check her arm again? To apologize again? Or to kiss her some more? She wasn't too proud to admit she hoped for the latter.

The icy look in his eyes made her think he'd returned for none of those reasons.

She sat frozen on her bed, the movie still playing on her computer sitting on her lap as he strode toward her. His gaze never leaving her face, Drew came to her bedside, then sat down, his hip pressed hard against hers.

She raised her brows high at him. What was he doing? His expression did not match his actions.

Still not saying a word, Drew dropped his gaze to her chest, making her skin prickle. Then he reached a hand toward the neckline of her sleep tee, and Peyton reflexively pressed herself back against her stacked pillows.

He paused. "Can I see?"

God, she hated this part. He appeared to know though, so there wasn't much point in refusing. She gave a short nod.

She watched in what seemed to her like slow motion as he hooked his index finger in the banded neckline of her T-shirt and gently eased it down, stretching it until he'd exposed her cleavage.

And her scar.

She looked up, and her gaze collided with his.

Yep, he knew.

She asked, "How?"

"Natalie." He lifted his other hand and ran his index and middle finger over the still faintly ridged scar.

The closed incision had flattened and faded considerably in the past fifteen years, but it remained obvious proof that she'd had her chest cracked open.

His gaze remaining on the scar and seemingly oblivious to the fact his knuckles were also brushing the inner curve of her breasts, he continued, "She'd wanted me to sign a release form so she could use the footage they shot of me checking on you in the sheep pen."

Peyton latched on to the distraction from his touch. "Did you sign it?"

He lifted his gaze to meet hers again. "No. I didn't." He removed his fingers from her chest and raised the neck of her T-shirt to where it belonged. Then he settled his hands on his muscular thighs. "I did watch the segment on you that they were in the process of editing, however."

Regret washing over her, Peyton closed her computer and set it aside. "I should have never accurately filled out that medical waiver."

Drew shifted on the bed to face her more fully. "That would have been dumb, Peyton, considering what the waiver was for."

"I know"—she huffed—"but I should have known Nat would use what was on it in the show. What exactly did she include in the segment?"

"Some photos of you as a child, before…"—he raised a hand and pointed at her chest—"and several as a teenager doing…a lot." He shook his head as if bemused. "She does a voice-over where she says you had open-heart surgery as a ten-year-old."

Which was correct, but not what she wanted to be known for. Not at all.

"So, what was it?" Drew asked softly.

Of course, he'd want to know the details. Peyton absently rubbed at the scar. "Patent foramen ovale."

"PFO," he murmured. "Not fun."

She nodded. A little hole between the left and right atria of her heart. A little hole capable of big problems. "I was born with it, obviously, but they didn't find it until I was ten."

"Do you know if they stitched or patched it?"

"Patch. My mom and dad are terrified I'll tear it."

Drew shook his head. "Assuming your docs knew what they were doing, I wouldn't worry about that."

"I guarantee my parents, as well as my grandparents, made sure I had the best in the field."

Drew nodded as if he completely understood, and she was reminded that he was from a family where money wasn't an issue, also. He must know that money also couldn't buy peace of mind when a loved one was sick or injured.

Feeling she might have an ally, for once, Peyton continued, "My entire family thinks the only way to keep me healthy is to treat me like a china doll, despite what the doctors told them. My brothers, in particular, would be happiest if I was kept locked away, with no real life at all."

Drew reached out a hand and adjusted the ice pack on her shoulder, squeezing it as if testing if she needed fresh ice or not. "You can't blame them. It's very hard on a family when someone they love is sick or injured." He said it as if he had personal experience. Undoubtedly, as a doctor, even one not yet finished with his training, he'd encountered plenty of distressed family members of sick—or more likely in the rodeo world, injured—people.

Apparently not liking the feel of her ice pack, he plucked it from her arm and pushed off from the bed. He opened the small trailer's little refrigerator and opened the freezer shelf, finding the bag of ice she kept stuffed inside. He dumped the partially melted ice from the bag into the sink.

While he refilled the ice bag, he asked, "When was the last time you saw your heart surgeon?"

She sighed. Here it came. The moment people found out about her heart she ceased being just Peyton and became Peyton's leaky heart. "Seeing as the operation was fifteen years ago, and he was the most experienced in his field at the time, my surgeon has long since retired."

"Of course." Drew came back to her, screwing the cap on the now full ice bag. "You must have been referred to someone else though."

She rolled her eyes to the trailer ceiling. "Yes."

"And?"

Her exasperation growing, she met his blue eyes squarely. "And do you really think my family would let me go without having a checkup before I left town?"

He shrugged. "They did insist that you were watched over by someone from sports medicine." He sat down again on the edge of the bed, his hips nestled against hers, and gingerly returned the ice bag to her shoulder. He took the time to position it so that the bruised part of her upper arm would be iced, also.

She watched his intent, handsome face. So handsome. So serious. His concern was genuine, as if he really cared. "But not to be my doctor, Drew."

His gaze jumped to hers. "Trust me, I don't want to be your doctor, Peyton." His gaze dropped to her mouth.

The heart in question started pounding in Peyton's chest. She'd never wanted to be kissed by a man so badly in her entire life.

But instead of kissing her again, he said, "I think I better go."

"Do you?"

His gaze met hers again. How could she have ever thought him cold? Fire danced in his blue eyes, hypnotic with a heady mix of need and passion.

"Yes. Because of your arm."

She didn't believe him. "Just my arm?"

He smiled. Peyton decided she wanted to make him smile a lot more.

"Yes. I need to go." But instead of standing again, he leaned toward her and captured her mouth with his.

This time his kiss was less tentative and more…claiming. Definitely more certain. He kissed her hard and deeply and as if he intended to kiss her a whole hell of a lot more.

Peyton loved it. She reached for him to pull him closer, but he broke off the kiss and moved away. She felt the loss all the way to the bottoms of her bare soles.

Standing, he repeated, "I have to go. Keep that ice on your arm, and we'll see how it looks in the morning."

"But you are not my doctor, Drew."

He smiled again. "No, ma'am. I am not your doctor." He retrieved his hat from the table, replaced it on his head, then tugged on the brim by way of goodbye before leaving her trailer.

Peyton dropped her head back on the pillows. Oh boy.

She didn't just like that guy. She liked him *a lot*. And she wanted him. The most cautious guy around. And a doctor to boot.

She covered her face with a pillow and stifled a scream of frustration.

CHAPTER THIRTEEN

THOUGH HE'D ENDED the night before in Peyton's trailer with nothing more than a kiss because of her injury, Drew realized he had an obvious spring in his step the next morning as he made his way from the sports medicine trailer to where Peyton's little trailer was parked. He'd had a terrible night's sleep—or was it a good night?—thinking about kissing Peyton Halliday. Among other things.

He just couldn't get the feel of her, the taste of her, out of his head. And by dawn, he'd decided he didn't want to.

Because Doc Tracer wasn't going to let Drew work in the clinic until Peyton left with the other women for the next region on their exhibition tour—something Drew would have to face when it happened—he'd decided to check on her arm and shoulder in *a not her doctor* capacity, then ask if she'd like to drive down to see Crater Lake with him. If she'd thought Smith Rock had been amazing, then she would be down for seeing the deepest lake in the nation.

And the roughly two-and-a-half-hour drive both ways would give him focused time with her and go a long way toward keeping her from physical harm for the day. A win-win as far as Drew was concerned.

When he reached her trailer, a place he was really starting to like, he rapped on the door. She didn't answer. Drew knocked again, and when she still didn't answer, he tried the latch.

Locked.

Oh boy. Peyton Halliday was on the loose.

Then he remembered Peyton mentioning the veritable breakfast bar that Natalie laid out every morning for the cast and crew. Peyton had probably gone to the big RV for something to eat. Another apple fritter sounded pretty good to Drew, also.

He wove his way around the other competitors' traveling homes until he reached the row where the *Buckin' TV* rig was parked. He arrived just in time to see a veritable flood of cowgirls including Peyton leaving the RV, laughing and chattering as usual, followed by the TV crew, Natalie…and Alec.

What was his little brother doing with the Buckin' Babes?

Drew stopped and pulled in a breath. Talk about a stupid question. A group of beautiful women, his unattached hound dog of a little brother…of course Alec was hanging out here.

The group turned toward the large passenger van they used to ferry the group around whatever town they happened to be visiting. Alec's truck was parked next to the van, and he seemed to be directing Nat to follow him.

Alarm set Drew in motion toward the group. Alec was a bull rider. Doing risky things was how he rolled. If he'd come up with something for the women to be filmed doing, the odds of it being something Peyton's family wouldn't want her doing—what *he* wouldn't want her doing, he realized with a jolt—was pretty close to one hundred percent.

Alec noticed him trotting toward them. "Hey, Drew." Alec raised a hand in greeting, his devil-may-care smile wide.

Out of the corner of his eye, Drew saw Peyton pause to watch him and Alec. The morning sun glinting in her copper hair threatened to totally derail him, but he needed to find out what Alec had cooked up first.

Drew beckoned his little brother to him.

"You have perfect timing. I was just about to call you," Alec said.

"What are you up to?" Drew asked, struggling to keep from looking back at Peyton. She pulled him to her as if she had a lead on him. In equal measures an annoying and thrilling sensation.

"Just being brilliant," Alec said with a smug look and crossed his arms over his chest, obviously pleased with himself.

"Considering you spend your days being dumped on your head—"

"I wear a helmet."

"Still, your definition of brilliant might be different from mine."

Alec rolled his eyes. "Yeah, whatever. Anyway, I invited the Buckin' Babes to come to our ranch and see firsthand how the broncs they ride are raised, cared for, and trained."

"Did you clear the visit with Grandfather and Ian?"

Alec gave Drew a *duh* look. "Yes. It will be great publicity for Liam's bronc program and for the Wright Ranch brand overall. Plus, we'll get to spend the day with the Babes." He rocked back on his boot heels.

Drew smiled, relieved. "That is kinda brilliant, Alec. We can easily keep them busy for the day. The *whole* day." He clapped a hand down on Alec's shoulder and turned him toward where the women were loading into the van. Peyton seemed to be hovering outside, delaying climbing in with the other women. She kept glancing toward Drew and Alec.

Was she worried he didn't want her to see his home? Or was she concerned he regretted kissing her last night? Again. He'd have to make sure she knew neither was true.

"Can I ride with you?" he asked Alec.

"Figured you would."

As Drew walked toward the van and Alec's truck, he gave Peyton a small smile and tugged at the brim of his hat.

Her shoulders relaxed and one corner of her luscious mouth inched upward. She watched him long enough to heat his blood before she turned and climbed into the van.

Maybe he'd have to reassure her in a private place.

Alec laughed. "Wow, Drew. I've never seen you look at anything but a medical text book like that. Could it be you've finally decided to appreciate the human body for something other than clinical study?"

"Shut up, Alec," Drew said without heat.

He did the opposite, laughing hard as he climbed into the driver's seat. "Yes! Welcome to the world of the living."

Fastening his seat belt, Drew asked, "Did you clear this with Liam, too?"

Alec made a hedging sound as he pulled forward, gesturing out of his open window for the van to follow him. "I figure it might be better to ask for forgiveness instead of permission."

Drew snorted. "Forgiveness from Liam? You do like to court death, don't you?"

Alec shrugged but grinned unrepentantly.

It hit Drew that Alec and Peyton were a lot alike. They both had reacted to something traumatic in their lives by becoming daredevils.

Drew had done the exact opposite. Instead of throwing care to the wind, he'd armed himself with the knowledge he'd need to make sure he never lost anyone he loved again. At least as much as humanly possible. He suddenly realized he'd dealt with the rest, what was beyond human control, by simply keeping himself apart. Unseen. Because there was less risk that way. So far, his approach to life had worked just fine for him.

But maybe not so much now. Since a certain redhead had entered the picture.

He leaned so he could see into the truck's large, passenger-side mirror, checking to make sure the big white passenger van was following the black Wright Ranch truck that Alec used.

The sight of the van directly behind them instantly put him at ease. Peyton was there, right behind him, on her way to what he considered the safest place on earth. Despite the

LEAH VALE

fact it was where his mother had been injured and ultimately died. But he considered the Wright Ranch to be so safe now because every person living and working there had been touched by his mother's death, and he trusted them to never let something so devastating happen again.

Out of the corner of his eye, Drew caught Alec repeatedly looking at him as he drove toward home, so he finally asked, "What?"

"Haven't seen you hanging on the fence with Doc these past few days."

"Doc gave me an assignment that has taken me away from the arena."

"Oh yeah?" Alec shifted in his seat, his curiosity tangible.

"Yeah." Drew wasn't about to tell Alec about Peyton. It would be all over the entire rodeo by the end of the day.

"This assignment wouldn't happen to have anything to do with a very pretty, not to mention badass, little redhead, would it?"

Drew shot his brother a look. "What makes you think that?"

Alec tilted his head back and forth in the annoying way he did when he had something on one of his older siblings. "Oh, I don't know, maybe because I know you were spotted lurking outside her trailer, and then again going in and out of it."

Drew huffed out a breath. "Yeah, okay. My assignment has to do with Peyton Halliday."

Alec scoffed. "I know you're a dyed in the wool stick in the mud and all, but I can't believe you'd call that smokin' hot firecracker an assignment. Geez, Drew."

Drew had had enough. He turned toward the brother he'd always been closest to and told him the truth. "Her family has offered to pay for significant upgrades and additional funding for the sports medicine clinic program. And if you want to have the best immediate medical aid next time you get busted up after coming off a bull wrong, then I'm expected to keep that smokin' hot firecracker safe while she's here in Pineville."

Alec gave a silent *oh*, then turned his attention back to the road. The silence lasted barely a heartbeat before Alec glanced back at Drew and said, "Probably because she's the sort who'd try to climb on a bull like Red Rum."

Drew gave an exaggerated nod. "Probably."

Alec matched his nod for a moment, then added, "She sure is cute though."

Drew turned his attention to the road in front of them. "Yeah. She is." Cute and sweet and funny and smart.

If only what he could accomplish in the future wasn't dependent on her acting completely opposite to her nature for her family's peace of mind.

PEYTON HAD TO admit she was as excited to visit the Wright Ranch as the other women in the van, but certainly for much different reasons. It wasn't Thomas Wright's wealth, obvious from the moment the van followed Alec Neisson's truck through the giant, elaborately scrolled wrought iron gate and started up the long, blacktopped drive, that piqued her interest. It was the fact that Thomas Wright was Drew's grandfather.

She was eager to see where Drew's caring, tenacious character had formed. To better know the man whose kiss she couldn't stop thinking about.

At first Peyton had been worried when Alec had shown up without Drew at the *Buckin' TV* RV with the offer to visit their family home. Drew didn't strike her as the type to want to expose their home to a *check out my crib* sort of reality TV moment. But then he'd shown up as they were leaving and sent her a smile and hat tip that had gone a long way toward reassuring her.

As well as made her heart do a funny thump in her chest. Just as a single kiss from him did funny things to other parts of her.

So now she was going to see his home. Along with a chattering gaggle of other women, but still. And they probably would only go into the stables, but for those who grew up on a working ranch, the stables and barns were the heart of the home.

As she suspected, Alec's truck bypassed the circular drive in front of the large home that looked more like a mountain resort lodge than a single-family dwelling. Nat was pointing and rattling off several different shot angles she wanted with clear excitement.

Several of the women squealed at the sight of a life-sized bronze sculpture of a rearing horse in the center of the circular drive. Nearly all of them held up their phones to take a picture of the horse. Peyton didn't. She'd grown up with a life-sized bronze sculpture of a Texas longhorn bull that her grandfather had had commissioned. Maybe the statues meant the grandfathers had something in common? Why she cared was beyond her.

She might not even see any other members of Drew's family beside his affable younger brother, but the possibility didn't stop her palms from sweating.

The vehicles continued around the big house, which appeared to be made up of a large center section with two single-story wings jutting out on either side. They parked in front of a huge, multi-bayed garage off to the side of the home. There were no other cars or trucks parked in the large blacktopped area between the garage and house, but with a garage that size, there were plenty of places to park inside. It didn't mean no one was here.

Before exiting the van, she rubbed her hands on her jeans as best she could with her sore shoulder in an attempt to dry her palms.

Thank goodness she had wiped her hands off because Drew was there waiting outside the van, a hand outstretched to help the ladies from the van in true cowboy fashion. Though she absolutely didn't need any help stepping out of a van any more than the other girls did, she slipped the hand of her uninjured arm into his and allowed Drew to balance her as she stepped to the asphalt.

Steeling herself for the impact of his blue eyes, she raised her gaze to his. And found his attention on her hurt arm. He was playing not-her-doctor doctor. He proved it by retaining her hand and gently pulling her away from the group.

She blew out a breath. "I'm fine, Drew."

"Just taking a quick peek." He raised the sleeve of her *I Love Texas* short-sleeve T-shirt, which she'd worn specifically on the chance he'd do exactly this, and gently turned her arm to better see the purple bruise.

"Not my doctor, Drew."

That brought his gaze up to hers. The heat she'd expected before was there, and more than just her palms began to sweat.

One corner of his mouth curled upward. "Not your doctor, Peyton." Despite the statement, he looked back down at her arm, gently probing the bruised area. "Consider me a concerned friend who just happens to have a medical degree."

The thought of having Drew as a friend unfurled something in her chest. Especially if he turned into a friend with benefits.

Luckily oblivious to the path her thoughts were tripping down, he nodded his approval. "The swelling has decreased considerably. How's the pain?"

"Only hurts when some random doctor pokes at it." She smiled up at him.

He chuckled, lowering her sleeve and smoothing it in place. "Some random doctor, huh? I'll keep my eye out for him."

"Appreciate it." Peyton was pretty sure she was going to have a hard time keeping her eyes off said doctor, especially when he smiled the way he currently was.

Behind her, Peyton heard Nat say, "That's perfect. You got it?"

"Got it."

Peyton turned and found Dan still looking through the camera viewfinder, the lens aimed squarely at her and Drew.

"Excellent." Nat definitely sounded smug.

Peyton turned back to Drew. His gaze was on Nat and her cameraman, his mouth no longer smiling.

Regret for exposing him in a way she knew he didn't want made Peyton reach for him.

He slid his hand down to her elbow and gave her arm one final squeeze before releasing her. "I didn't sign the release, remember? Don't worry."

He stepped away from her and said, "The bronc barn is this way, ladies and gentlemen." He started walking in the direction Alec and most of the ladies were already heading.

Peyton watched him go, wondering at his ability to…settle her, like an overexcited animal, in a way no one she'd ever met before could. She liked it.

Looking very much like a pied piper, Alec was leading the group of women past the smallest and fanciest barn, built and finished to match the main house. Nat and her two-man crew were running to catch up with them. Peyton hurried to catch up with Drew.

When she reached his side, she asked, "Not the bronc barn?"

He shook his head. "Not the bronc barn. Saddle horses."

They approached the largest barn, which was much more utilitarian, but Alec kept the group moving with a steady commentary Peyton couldn't quite hear.

She looked questioningly at Drew. "Not the bronc barn?"

He shook his head, but a smile was teasing at his mouth again. "Not the bronc barn. Bulls."

She took in the size of the structure and whistled. "That's a lot of bull."

"There are cows and steer in there, too. And one of my grandfather's offices."

Curiosity flaring, Peyton looked toward the huge, mostly metal barn again. Was Thomas Wright in there right now, pouring over breeding books in an attempt to create the next biggest, baddest bull that his brand was so famous for? She suddenly itched to get a closer look. While she'd always figured she would someday use her psychology degree by getting trained and certified to be a counselor, maybe helping kids who found themselves stuck in hospitals, she wouldn't mind dabbling in bull or bronc breeding. Someday.

She must have paused because Drew settled a warm hand on her back and urged her forward.

As they walked, he pointed toward one of two remaining barns, this one medium in size compared to the first two. "That's the bronc barn."

Peyton nodded toward the last, classic style barn. "And that barn? Please don't tell me you have sheep."

He laughed. "No, we don't raise sheep. That's the old barn. It's for equipment and storage."

"Y'all have a lot of barns."

He shrugged. "It's my grandfather's life's work."

Peyton's grandfather's life's work was built on dead dinosaurs.

She took in the beauty of the ranch, from the beautifully designed and maintained barns and outbuilding, to the lush green irrigated pastures, and on to the snow-capped mountain range that provided a frame to it all. "It's so gorgeous here."

"I haven't been able to give it up."

A short, sharp whistle sounded behind them. They stopped and turned toward the sound. A tall, broad-shouldered man with sun bleached blond hair stood on the edge of a large patio out the back of the main house and beckoned Drew with a wave.

"That's my oldest brother Ian. Apparently, he wants to talk to me." Drew hesitated for a moment as if debating bringing her to meet his brother.

As much as Peyton had been hoping to meet Drew's family, she chickened out. "Go. I'd better catch up with the girls to make sure that the only footage Nat has of me on this trip isn't what she shot of us."

That seemed to settle his internal debate for him. He gave a quick nod. "Okay. I'll catch up with you."

Peyton couldn't help but watch him jog away. For a guy who had to have spent most of his time with his nose in a book, he sure had a great body. Ranch strong, not gym thick. She knew from touching his shoulders, chest and arms that his muscles were long and sinewy, and it didn't take too much imagination to picture what they'd look and feel like without his shirt between them.

Afraid of where her hormones would take her thoughts next, Peyton turned and hurried to the bronc barn.

Which turned out to be mostly empty of broncs. Alec was unnecessarily explaining that with it being rodeo season, their best broncs, which was most of them, were contracted out. Like Karen From Finance was currently still at High Desert Rodeo grounds. Peyton automatically looked for Mustard Gas. He didn't seem to be in any of the stalls or attached paddocks. A stinky horse like that probably had to be kept in a very open pasture.

Having grown up on a similarly high-end ranch, Peyton quickly grew bored with Alec's rudimentary explanation of their program. The other girls didn't seem to mind, though, being more than impressed by Alec's charm.

Peyton was far more interested in what Drew was doing. She'd made sure to be front and center for at least a couple of the panning shots Nat favored. Telling herself she was simply saving Drew the trip to catch up with her, Peyton slipped out of the bronc barn.

But as she started toward the big house, she began to waver. This was their home. She didn't have the right to saunter up there. A little kissing didn't equal an invitation to meet the fam. And if she and Drew were to take their physical relationship further? Well, she'd deal with it if—or when—it happened.

She changed course and instead wandered to the bull barn. Much like the bronc barn and undoubtedly for the same reason, the paddocks and the attached stalls on the side of the barn appeared mostly empty. An equally empty corral was connected to the closest end of the barn, and rather than skirt it, Peyton decided to climb through the railing and walk across so she could check to see if the paddocks on the other side of the barn were empty too.

She was only a few paces inside the corral when she heard a yell from the direction of the house. She spotted Drew running toward her, gesturing at her.

"Peyton! Get out of that corral."

She instinctively looked around her, checking the door that the bulls would use to access the corral from the barn. She was completely alone in the circular space.

Then she realized she might have committed a transgression of some sort and hurried to retrace her steps.

She was just easing her way back through the fence rails when Drew reached her and practically hoisted her the rest of the way through the fence.

She was about to make a joke about threading a needle when she caught sight of his face. He was pale, and his jaw was clenched. But the worst was the look in his eyes. He almost looked panicked. She could plainly see what had to be fear, stark and wild, creating a storm with his blue eyes.

Peyton couldn't help but look behind her again. The corral was still empty of any sort of danger.

Drew started to grab her by the shoulders but stopped, apparently in deference to her bruised arm.

He fisted his hands and dropped them to his sides, instead. "Don't ever go inside that corral."

"I'm sorry. But I'd just wanted to see—"

"Ever, Peyton. Do you understand?"

LEAH VALE

A deep voice behind her said, "Drew."

As Drew straightened, Peyton turned. The man standing at the corner of the barn outside the corral could only be Thomas Wright.

He gave a two-finger beckon then retreated back around the corner of the barn. His office must be on that side.

Drew said, "Stay right here. Please." Without waiting for her to say anything, he trotted around the perimeter of the corral and disappeared where his grandfather had gone.

"You have to forgive Drew," an equally deep but less gruff voice said.

She spun to find the man who'd whistled Drew to the house, his oldest brother Ian. The family resemblance was obvious in the stupid good looks, but Ian was bigger, more weathered. And his eyes were a darker blue than Drew's, yet no less intense and knowing.

She asked, "What did I do?"

"Nothing, really." Ian hooked his thumbs in his jeans' pockets. "But something pretty bad happened in that corral, and it spooks some members of the family in different ways."

"What happened?"

He ran his disconcerting gaze over her for a moment, then said, "Have Drew tell you. Least he can do after hollering at you."

Knowing it was much easier to run from pretty bad things than stand around talking about them, she nodded vaguely. As much as she burned to know more about Drew, she wasn't about to get her hopes up.

"So, you ride broncs?" Ian reclaimed her attention.

"Ranch saddle broncs," she clarified.

"Just as impressive," he asserted in a way that made her instantly like him. "Has Drew told you about his nemesis, Buckaroo Bonsai?"

Her curiosity flared white hot again. "He has not."

Ian's handsome smile grew wide. "Now that's a story I can tell you."

CHAPTER FOURTEEN

WHEN DREW LEFT his grandfather's office in the bull barn, still smarting from the chewing out he'd received for raising his voice to a lady, especially a lady he'd been tasked with treating with kid gloves, he found Peyton standing in the exact spot he'd told her to stay in.

Laughing with Ian.

A prickling of unease, or maybe even jealousy, had Drew breaking into a trot as he rounded the corral. A totally ridiculous sensation considering Ian was happily married to Jessie, a stunningly beautiful badass FBI special agent.

But nothing about Drew's ever-growing attraction to the woman he was supposed to be watching over made sense. Looking at her though, completely at ease, laughing with his very intimidating oldest brother, his attraction made perfect sense. She was beautiful, smart, fun, and brave.

Drew had no choice but to recognize that he was in deep. And all the years he had worked toward one goal, taking over the sports medicine clinic and keeping himself safe from the kind of pain his mother's death had wrought, were about to go into the dirt.

Ian and Peyton broke off from whatever they'd been

talking about when he approached them.

Drew's anxious curiosity must have shown on his face because Peyton rushed to explain. "Your brother was just telling me about your attempts to ride Buckaroo Bonsai."

Drew rolled his eyes. Buckaroo Bonsai was the name they'd given an empty fifty-gallon barrel Ian had strung between two Aspen trees with some rope when they were kids. They'd pretended the barrel was a bucking bull and had delighted in tugging on the ropes to fling whichever sibling was aboard into the dirt. "Let's just say there's a reason I went into medicine instead of bull or bronc riding."

He'd been thinking of his inability to stay aboard the barrel, but the quick look Ian and Peyton exchanged made his breath catch in his throat. Had Ian been telling darker tales?

Peyton met his gaze and distracted him with a bright smile. "We had an actual mechanical bull, like the kind they have in bars, to play on growing up. But we weren't clever enough to name it."

Drew blinked. That explained a lot about her ability to stay on mounts like Karen From Finance.

"It was supposed to be just for my three older brothers, but…" She trailed off with a guilty shrug.

Drew could easily imagine Peyton as a young girl, thumbing her nose at anyone who tried to tell her she had to stay away from the bucking machine. She had a rebellious streak as wide as the Rio Grande and the backbone to take on any challenge. The man who harnessed all that energy would have his hands full. He swallowed hard. Not him. He couldn't. Could he?

Ian said, "Well, I'd better get back to my paperwork. It was a pleasure to meet you, Peyton. Hopefully I'll be seeing you around." He tipped his hat to the petite redhead then sent Drew a *don't screw this up* look before walking away.

But don't screw what up? The funding for the clinic upgrade by not keeping Peyton safe? Or whatever it was that was growing between them?

His gut churned. He couldn't fail. On both counts. The clinic needed the additional funding, and he would do anything to keep from hurting Peyton. Even if that meant holding back and sticking to keeping things professional.

When he shifted his attention from Ian's retreating back to Peyton, he found her watching him, her gaze searching. All because he hadn't been able to stay on a bouncing barrel? How would she look at him if Ian had told her some of the less pleasant stories from their childhood?

His heart stuttered. What if Ian had told her? "Did you and Ian talk about anything else?"

"He said you needed to tell me what happened in this corral." She reached a hand to pat at the nearest rail.

Drew swallowed hard. The dark tale he hated the most. As much as he'd like to take a hard pass, he'd learned enough about Peyton to know she wouldn't let it slide if he refused. He reached for the same corral rail to anchor himself. "Our mother was trampled by a bull in there. It took a very long time, but the injuries eventually killed her."

Peyton clapped a hand over her mouth.

"I was pretty young, and blessedly didn't see it happen,

but I spent a lot of time in the corner of the room here at the house my dad and grandfather outfitted for her to be cared for in. I guess it left a mark."

Peyton reared back as if understanding had hit her like a spray of dirt. "And made you want to become a doctor."

Drew nodded. "Not much mystery there."

Peyton turned and stared at some spot within the corral.

The true mystery was how he was going to be able to keep from wanting her to sooth that mark.

The sound of Alec, still playing the role of tour guide while leading the group of women and the camera crew back toward where the van and truck were parked, reached them, giving Drew a reprieve from his thoughts and drawing Peyton's attention from the corral.

She looked to him, stepped forward, and settled a small hand on his chest. Her fingers flexed slightly. "I better get back to the group." She patted his chest, but the pat turned into a caress.

His blood surged from the point of contact outward until his knees threatened to buckle. Heat charged through his veins like a horse released from a chute, and every nerve ending stood at attention wanting to be caressed, too. God, he wanted to kiss her again.

He captured her hand in his, holding her palm against his chest. How would the hot touch of her hand feel without a shirt? Skin on skin. His mouth went dry. "See you back at the RV?"

Her fingers flexed slightly on his pec again. Would she grip his back that way, too?

She said, "Wait for me at my trailer?"

She was waiting for him to agree, but all he could manage was a short nod because his throat had closed up on him.

Her fingers flexed yet again on his chest then she slipped her hand from beneath his and walked away.

And he watched every sway. She flipped her hair over her shoulder and glanced back at him. The gleam in her hazel eyes let him know she was very aware he was watching her. Minx.

Alec's toothy whistle yanked him out of her hypnotic thrall. He looked toward his little brother near the vehicles. "You want to go back to the rodeo grounds with me?"

He signaled he did with a wave and a lift of his chin. It was barely noon, but surely he'd be able to come up with something to do with Peyton, in her trailer, that would keep her from harm's way for the rest of the day.

Some of those possibilities had him rethinking his plan as he watched her climb into the van. Being alone with her might be more hazardous than he wanted to tempt.

"THAT'S A LOOK I've never seen on your face before," Sammie said as Peyton squeezed onto the rear-most van bench seat next to her.

Though she wasn't exactly sure what look Sammie was referring to, Peyton tried to school her features into a guileless expression. "I have no idea what you're talking about."

Sammie snorted loudly, then shot a glance toward the front of the van where Nat was settling into the passenger seat right before the van started up. "Granted, I was mostly babysat by my oldest cousin Charlotte, but I've never had the urge to touch my babysitter like you were touching Doc Cowboy."

"I was just patting him on the chest because he was being a good boy." She tried to play off what she'd done, but the heat was already creeping up her neck, and her gaze automatically went to the big pickup truck pulling onto the drive ahead of them.

"Then that's one very good boy. What'd he do?"

Peyton shrugged, struggling to put the feelings Drew stirred in her to words. "He was sweet." Sweet and scarred. Her equally scarred heart gave a telling *bump*.

Sammie narrowed her eyes at Peyton. "You know, falling in love with a certain cold fish might be your greatest adventure of all, Miss Crazy Pants."

Peyton knew she was in deep shit because the only thought that popped into her head was *Drew is so not a cold fish*. She shifted her gaze out the van window, trying to think about the beautiful scenery passing by but only able to think about Drew. The way he kissed her, the heat he'd generated between them, she'd never experienced anything so hot before. And he was not the first cowboy she'd kissed. But the others had been the type who were good with superficial. Temporary. Drew didn't strike her as the same type.

Plus, he was overly cautious. Thanks to what he had just told her at the prompting of his oldest brother, Peyton knew

Drew had a very, very compelling reason to be cautious. And to avoid becoming involved with someone like her. She didn't feel as if she was living if she wasn't taking a chance of some sort. Drew clearly wanted to avoid the potential cost of those risks. She truly couldn't blame him.

The fact that she'd be gone from his life in a few days' time was a good thing because she had no intention of changing how she lived her life. She also had enough people already in her life fussing over her, telling her not to do this, not to do that. She didn't need to add Drew to the list.

The knowledge didn't stop her pulse from spiking when the van pulled into its parking space next to the *Buckin' TV*'s RV, and Drew and Alec were there waiting to help the ladies exit the van.

The minute she slipped her hand into Drew's, and he curled his fingers around hers, the heat from his palm soaking into every inch of her, she admitted she very much wanted Drew squarely at the top of the list.

At least for today.

The fact that he kept hold of her hand and moved with her away from the van, leaving Sammie to be helped out by a very pleased looking Alec, made her think maybe he felt the same way.

At least for today.

Though she hadn't been very old when she'd been sick, she'd promised herself she would live every day without worrying about the next. That she would do her best to live. And that's what she would do with Drew.

At least for today.

So, when he said, "Now what?" clearly expecting she'd have something wild and crazy planned for the substantial chunk of time before the exhibition rides, she smiled and shifted her hand within his so that she could thread her fingers through his just like he'd done when they'd been walking the trail at Smith Rock.

"I was planning on going back to my trailer." She'd said the words with breezy confidence, but her heart was now pounding. Normally, she'd celebrate the resulting rush of adrenaline, but not now. She had to admit her concern stemmed from the fact that she liked Drew too much. Maybe he'd take the opportunity presented by her inactivity to go back to the clinic trailer where his actual job was.

And leave her to contemplate why she was so attracted to the man.

He glanced down at her, his eyes questioning. Uncertain. "Would you like some company?"

A shiver of need coursed over her, and she had to work hard not to melt against him.

Just for today, she amended her mantra.

She met his stunning blue gaze and said, "Only if it's you."

Surprise flared in his eyes, then was followed by a heat so intense she thought she might incinerate on the spot. His mouth settled into a determined line. He gave her hand a squeeze, then pulled her forward as he increased his pace.

She laughed. "What are you doing?"

"Making sure I get you out of sight before your producer and her crew decide to join us."

"That would be a different sort of reality TV," she said on another laugh as they rounded a camper parked at the end of the row between her trailer and the crew's RV.

Drew stumbled, and Peyton blanched at having said the words in her outside-of-her-head voice.

But instead of yanking his hand away and getting all I'm-not-that-sort-of-guy on her, Drew shocked her by pulling her to him and scooping her up into his arms with a hand behind her knees and the other behind her back. She'd been right about him being ranch strong.

She squeaked and wrapped an arm around his neck. "What are you doing now?"

"Making sure you don't get away from me."

Her heart gave another one of those *bumps*. She placed her other hand over the one gripping his strong, hot neck. "Why would you think I would try to do that?"

"Worst-case scenario thinker." He sent her a wink.

"That does not surprise me. And I'm good with it, by the way."

At least for today.

"I'm glad. Because that's one thing I doubt I'd be able to change. My hair color though…" He trailed off teasingly as he carried her to her trailer door.

"Don't even joke." She released his neck and fished in her front jeans pocket for the door key.

Drew bent his knees so she could reach to insert the key into the lock. "Got a thing for blonds?"

She met his gaze. "Just one." She pressed the latch and opened the door.

"Hopefully, it's me because turns out I have a serious thing for redheads."

"All redheads?"

"Just one."

Her heart feeling as if it might burst, for once in a good way, Peyton pulled open the trailer door wide enough for them to enter. Drew stepped up into the trailer, turned, and in a feat of balance that had her laughing, hooked the door handle with the toe of his cowboy boot and pulled the trailer door closed with a slam.

"That would have been a lot easier if you had put me down."

"But what's the fun in that?"

"Dr. Drew putting fun over practicality? Be still my heart."

Drew paused, slipping his arm from behind her knees and returning her to her feet. Though he kept hold of her with his hands on her ribs just below her breasts, he stepped back. "About that."

"Fun over practicality?"

"Your heart. Have you been cleared for—"

"Sex?" She regained the step he'd taken back from her. "Drew, I wouldn't zip line if I couldn't knock boots."

A smile tugged at his mouth, but he was clearly doing his best to remain serious. He reached up and pulled her cowboy hat from her head as well as his own, dropping them both on the dinette table.

"But why are your family members so concerned about you?"

"Especially since, as you pointed out, the odds of my heart surgeon being a hack are pretty slim?" She shrugged and stepped away from him to face the bed. "I was a sick little kid for a hot minute. It scared them."

He moved to stand directly behind her. "But now you're okay."

His heat and intoxicatingly masculine smell had her swaying back against him. "I know that, and you know that. Mainly because you have a medical degree."

Drew slid his hands around her waist, spreading his hands wide and pulling her to him. "Considering we're the only ones here at the moment..."

Her patched heart soared. Peyton tilted her head back, exposing her neck. Drew obliged by nuzzling the tender skin beneath her ear then placed kisses down the side of her neck. She covered his hands with hers and drew them upward to her breasts. Drew groaned, and the sound and sensation of his touch set off fireworks inside her.

She turned her head and found his mouth with hers, kissing him deeply and with all the need he'd ignited in her.

Drew slipped his hands from beneath hers and found the hem of her T-shirt, easing it upward.

He was so cautious. Bless his heart.

Peyton yanked her T-shirt the rest of the way off and turned within his arms to start on the buttons of his shirt. She wanted this. She wanted this with Drew. And she wanted it now.

Drew got the memo and started unfastening his belt and jeans as he toed off his boots. He shucked his jeans and underwear down his legs. He was more glorious than she could have ever imagined.

Peyton did the same with her boots, but before she could peel off her own jeans, Drew wrapped his arms around her and carried her to the bed, shuffling with his jeans wrapped around his ankles.

Peyton reflexively wrapped her arms around his neck. She liked this guy. Really, really liked this guy. In a way she'd never felt before. And that both thrilled and scared her. Much like zip-lining down a mountain but without the assurance of safety equipment.

When Drew reached the bed, he laid her gently down on the mattress, kicking his way out of his jeans and boxers. Then being the giver he was, he stripped her bra, jeans, and matching panties from her. He trailed kisses the entire way.

Peyton gasped from the explosion of sensation rocketing through her. "Okay, now you are just showing off your knowledge of anatomy."

He lifted his head, his pale blue eyes sparking fire. "Is it working?"

Peyton grounded herself with a hand against the trailer wall above her head. "Hell yeah, it's working. Don't stop."

He chuckled, breathing warm, moist air on some very sensitive parts. "Yes, ma'am."

Peyton smiled, breathing through the pleasure he was bathing her in, until she couldn't take it anymore. Burying her fingers in his hair, she pulled him upward. Drew crawled his way up her body, grazing her sensitive skin with his lightly haired chest.

He paused, reaching for his jeans. Hearing the rip of plastic, Peyton smiled. Always the caregiver. The spread of warmth and affection surprised the hell out of her.

Having spent the majority of her life being smothered because she'd been sick—okay, very sick—for a relatively short period of time, she'd made an art out of avoiding people who showed care and concern to the point of being annoying. But with Drew…with Drew it was different. She liked his brand of care. Liked it so much she thought she would explode with delight.

Even though he'd only started caring for her because he was being paid to keep her safe.

Then he was inside her body, and she didn't care. She didn't care what, or who, had brought them to this point. All that she cared about was that Drew Neisson made her feel loved. And she didn't want it to end.

DREW TUCKED PEYTON against him after making love until he was left breathless. He was struck by the thought he never wanted to let her go. Which was crazy. He'd sworn to himself he would never expose his heart to the kind of pain he'd experienced while watching his mother struggle to cling to life. He'd never wanted to risk feeling that kind of pain again.

But Peyton, with her crazy way of dealing with the near-death experience she'd had as a child, had somehow wormed her way into his heart.

With the rays of the late afternoon sun slanting through the small window above Peyton's bed, Drew pulled her as close as he dared without waking her, nuzzling his face into her thick, soft, sweet-smelling riot of red curls. How could he have been so stupid? How could he have allowed himself to fall so completely for a woman who could cost him the future he'd worked so hard for?

He'd been entrusted with keeping her safe by her family. Not to play house with her.

She wiggled her warm bottom against him, and he had no choice but to admit how he'd been so stupid.

Because he'd fallen for her. Plain and simple.

He made love to her again, this time with the slow care she deserved.

When he began to trail kisses down the scar between her breasts, she at first flinched away, obviously self-conscious of the ridged flesh, but he persisted. Drew did his damnedest to let her know how beautiful he thought her, and how her scar was nothing more than proof of how tough, brave, and resilient he thought her.

And how much he loved her.

CHAPTER FIFTEEN

HAVING FALLEN ASLEEP in Peyton's bed, Drew slowly emerged from the deepest rest he'd had in a very long time. Even before he opened his eyes, he was immediately struck by how dry his mouth was and how thirsty he felt. He was dehydrated. No great surprise, considering his recent output.

He smiled with an overabundance of self-satisfaction and reached for the cause of his dehydration. His hand encountered empty space then rumpled sheets. Cracking an eye open against the bright, evening sunlight slanting directly through the window over Peyton's bed, Drew looked for her.

She wasn't in the bed next to him. He ran a hand over the pillow and sheets. No residual warmth from Peyton's hot, smooth skin remained.

Lifting his head, Drew searched for her. The small trailer was empty save for him. Maybe she was in the trailer's tiny bathroom. The narrow door to the small space was closed.

"Peyton?" he called, wincing at how raspy his voice sounded.

Silence.

He rolled toward the edge of the disheveled bed and

looked for Peyton's jeans and boots on the white and gold flecked vinyl floor of her trailer. He only saw his own pants, boxers, boots, and shirt still scattered where he'd shed them. Though Peyton's *I Love Texas* T-shirt was draped over the back of the dinette bench seat. A bare hanger lay atop the table.

It hadn't been there before.

She'd dressed and left. Had she regretted what they'd done together? Regretted it so much that she'd slipped out after he'd dozed off?

His chest tightened with the possibility, and not just with his own pain from being rejected in such a way. The idea that he'd caused her any sort of pain caused his heart to contract.

Reaching for his jeans and boxers, Drew noticed her bucking saddle was missing from its stand at the front of the trailer. She'd left to ride.

Drew's stomach flipped. Worry, fear, disappointment that she hadn't wanted to stay with him all warred for the spotlight within him.

He checked his watch. The women's bronc riding exhibition would be starting in five minutes.

So much for giving Peyton something better to do than possibly hurting herself on a bucking bronc during the exhibition tonight. He might have failed at keeping his relationship with Peyton clinical, not personal, but he wasn't about to fail to keep her from physical harm. And not just because her family was holding the additional clinic funding over him.

Drew wanted her safe because he'd fallen in love with her.

The thought of Peyton being hurt stirred the same sort of bone-deep fears that had eaten away at him while watching his mother deteriorate over the years between her initial injury beneath the hooves of his grandfather's prized bull and her eventual death. Logically, he knew Peyton's obvious skill on the back of whatever bronc she'd drawn would help keep her safe, but he couldn't avoid being sucked in by her family's fear for her safety.

He needed to keep her from harm for his own sanity.

Scrambling up from the tousled bedding, Drew gathered the rest of his clothing and redressed as quickly as he could. He was spurred on by the muffled sound of the announcer's deep voice coming over the public address system. The women's exhibition must just be beginning. He hadn't missed it. He needed to be there. And not only because he was supposed to be stopping her for doing anything risky.

Because he loved her, he repeated the thought. Trying it out. Letting it sink in and settle.

Not just because she was an amazing lay. Which she was. Holy shit, she was. But she was so, so much more. Peyton Halliday was brash, fun, fearless, beautiful, and generally all around perfect, as far as he was concerned.

Stomping into his boots, Drew grabbed his cowboy hat from the table and hurried from the trailer, slamming the door shut behind him.

He jogged to the arena, listening hard to the announcer's voice, growing more distinct as Drew neared the arena, for any mention of Peyton Halliday. The roar of the crowd had him increasing his pace. Peyton, with her petite stature and wild red hair, had turned out to be a crowd favorite. Especially after she'd successfully ridden Karen From Finance during the first women's saddle bronc riding exhibition, so the cheers could easily be for her.

Rather than going to his and Doc's regular spot along the fence near the exit gate where they kept the backboard and medical kit, Drew charged up the steps to the catwalk above the bucking chutes. If he could, he would stop Peyton from riding. How, he had no idea.

Just as Drew reached the crowded space above the chutes, he heard the announcer ask the crowd to cheer on Peyton Halliday, who had a whole lot of Texas grit packed into a little package. Drew knew she was made up of a whole lot more. She was joy, and light, and a zest for life that could only be gained from a brush with death.

His heart in his throat, he shoved his way toward the chute with the most activity above it just in time to see Peyton settle into her saddle atop a big, brown and black bronc. He opened his mouth to shout at her to stop, but he caught sight of the sheer joy on her face. She really loved what she was doing.

Drew realized he wanted her to be happy. More than anything. If he had any hope of a life spent loving her, he had to have the courage to let her be who she wanted to be. And one thing she'd taught him was how to be courageous. He'd always thought having courage meant being able to hold on tight, but she'd shown him that real courage meant letting go and taking the risk to truly live.

So instead of stopping her, he bent over the chute rail, snagged the bucking rope and handed it to her.

Peyton took the rope and glanced up, her gaze colliding with his. She froze, a question clear in her hazel eyes.

He answered her by straightening and saying, "Go get 'em, tiger."

Her smile was the most beautiful thing he'd ever seen. Then she blew him a kiss, leaned back, raised the thickly braided bucking rope, gripped the saddle horn, and nodded.

The side gate on the chute was pulled open by a cowboy on the ground, and the big bronc Drew didn't recognize because it wasn't from the Wright Ranch exploded into the arena.

Peyton's form was perfect. She continued to lean back in the saddle despite the horse's attempts to pitch her forward, then the animal gave three stiff-legged hops before settling into a pattern of high, twisting kicks.

Peyton clung to the saddle like a tick despite the big gelding's efforts to shake her, and Drew found himself thinking maybe she hadn't been exaggerating when she'd claimed there wasn't a horse she couldn't successfully ride.

Drew leaned down to grip the top rail of the chute, willing the eight second buzzer to sound. It already felt like Peyton had been riding the bronc for an hour.

But rather than hearing the buzzer signifying the end of the ride, Drew heard a loud *snap*. He watched in stunned horror as Peyton came off the bronc, saddle and all. Her girth strap had broken, and there was obviously nothing

Peyton could do but release the bucking rope and ride the horse-less saddle to the dirt.

Drew had seen more than his fair share of wrecks in the rodeo arena, but none had stopped his heart the way Peyton's wreck did. Without a thought, he launched himself over the railing and landed in the chute, then immediately ran to where Peyton had come to rest on her side on the ground. The pickup riders were working to box the bronc between them and keep him away from where Peyton was laying unmoving on her side.

His heart pounding against his ribs, Drew went to his knees in the soft dirt and leaned over her, trying to see her face. Her long hair was in the way though, so he gently brushed it back. Her eyes were squeezed shut, and she was gasping for air.

Terror gripped Drew. "Peyton? Peyton honey, look at me. Where do you hurt? Peyton!"

"Can't. Breathe," she gasped out, her eyes still squeezed closed.

Drew suddenly couldn't breathe himself. Couldn't pull air into his own lungs. Couldn't think.

Above him, Doc Tracer said, "Girl's had the wind knocked out of her. Just roll her over and lift her by the buckle."

Terrified of hurting her, Drew said, "What if something's broken?"

Doc Tracer made an exasperated noise and bent forward, resting his hands on his knees. To Peyton, he said, "Anything broke, hon?"

Still struggling for breath, Peyton shook her head vigorously.

"See." Doc straightened with a groan. "Now roll her over."

With trepidation, Drew reached for her. Fortunately, she'd landed on the non-bruised shoulder, but Drew had to grip her by the side of her chest to ease her onto her back. The last thing he wanted was to risk hurting her more by grabbing the arm she'd hit in the sheep pen. She'd remained literally in the saddle, so he had to pull it carefully from between her legs, extracting her feet from the stirrups, and move it aside. Once she was on her back, Drew slid his fingers beneath the waistband of her jeans and lifted her enough that her lungs could expand and allow her to catch her breath.

The very low-tech medical treatment worked, and Peyton opened her eyes as she pulled in several gulps of air. He eased her back down and commenced looking for further injury.

As Drew felt her neck and collar bones, gently probing for fractures, Peyton sat up. "What happened?"

Doc moved so he could toe at her saddle. "This saddle looks like it's seen some good times. When did you last replace this girth strap?"

Peyton groaned and ran a hand across her forehead, smearing it with dirt. "Never."

"Well, you'll be doing it now because it snapped clean in two." Doc sent her a cheeky wink.

Peyton groaned again. "That's my lucky saddle." She

struggled to her feet, with Drew doing his best to help her without hurting her. Once standing, she brushed off her backside and her chaps.

Drew kept an arm around her, his throat unbearably tight. He should have tugged on the girth after handing her the bronc rope instead of basking in her smile.

"Until it wasn't," Doc quipped and picked up the saddle. "Let's get her out of the way before the next bronc comes tearing through here."

Debating whether or not to just pick her up and carry her, Drew hesitated.

Doc asked Drew, "Do *you* need a stretcher?"

Feeling his face flush at his ridiculous indecisiveness, Drew bent to catch her behind the knees.

Peyton dodged him. "Oh no you don't. I'm walking out of this arena like every other self-respecting bronc rider."

Doc chuckled and hoisted the saddle onto his shoulder. "I think she's fine. But feel free to take her to the clinic and check her out for your own peace of mind."

"I plan to," Drew said, keeping a hand on her slender back despite her efforts to avoid him. He reached to pluck her hat from the dirt, but she snagged it before he could.

"I'll keep this." Doc patted the saddle. "With me at our usual spot. You can collect it when you're done at the clinic."

Peyton smiled at him. "Thank you, Dr. Tracer."

He touched a finger to his hat in acknowledgment, then veered off to where sports medicine always watched the action.

Drew helped Peyton through an arena gate and steered

her toward the clinic trailer.

"I'm fine, you know."

"And *I'll* be fine once I've checked you out."

"You just checked me out, twice, earlier today," she grumbled.

Drew pulled up short. For the second time, he found himself wondering if she regretted what had happened between them? An entirely different sort of panic hit him.

After a couple of steps, she seemed to notice he wasn't walking next to her and stopped, too, turning to look at him.

His concern must have shown because her shoulders dropped, and she closed the space between them.

Placing a very dirty hand on his chest, directly over his pounding heart, she tilted her head back to look him in the eye. "Drew. I really, really liked the way you *checked me out* earlier."

"Just *liked?*"

She groaned and dropped her head back farther. Turning on her boot heel, she said, "Needy much?" as she marched away.

Drew stayed where he was as realization washed over him. He was needy. He needed to help, to fix, to be seen. By Peyton.

All the things he hadn't been able to do for his mother. And despite everything she'd been through, or maybe because of them, Peyton did not need him. Was that why she was the first woman he'd ever felt this way about?

Peyton stopped again and turned to consider him. Her lips pressed together. She retraced her steps again, her chaps flapping around her ankles. This time when she reached him, she fisted her hands in his shirt. "Drew Neisson, you can be as needy as you want. As long as you are only needy with me. Because I didn't just *like* how you checked me out. I *loved* it. I love you. I loved you even before what you did up there on the catwalk. Okay? There I said it."

She released his shirt and threw her hands up in the air, turned and stomped three steps away, then turned again and stomped back. "Of all the people I could decide to *love* being *checked out* by, of course it has to be the person my dad hired to babysit me. A doctor, for God's sake. And you only agreed to do it because you knew I needed it."

"That's not why I agreed to do it."

Peyton stilled. "Then why?"

He pointed at the clinic trailer. His pride and joy. "Because of that."

She blinked.

"It's in serious need of an upgrade. Somebody has to pay for that."

"I just assumed your family…" She broke off at the shake of his head. "Then…my family?"

"Yes. And the additional funds will provide some security for what I hope to be my life's work. Funds tied to me keeping you safe."

She gaped at him. "I'd assumed, after talking to my dad, that you were being directly paid—"

"Yet you still slept with me."

"My family bribed you, yet you still slept with *me*."

They stared at each other for a long moment. Drew had

no idea what was going on inside her brain. His was a riot of fear, worry, elation, but most of all hope.

Then the gold in her hazel eyes warmed, and a smile teased at her mouth. "I want to do it again, Drew."

Relief loosened his knees. "That makes two of us."

She settled her hands on his hips, tugging him lightly to her. "Lucky for you, I know a place."

He started to tumble into her seductiveness, but there were some things about a person that just couldn't be changed. And he wasn't entirely certain if he was man enough to accept the challenge, the risk, of loving Peyton despite the potential heartbreak.

NERVOUS SHE'D MADE the wrong move by revealing what she had to Drew, and by using sex to distract him, Peyton tugged on him in an attempt to start him walking in the direction of her trailer.

Drew didn't budge. "After I actually check you out. I still need to know you're okay, Peyton."

"I'm fine, Drew."

"Then this won't take but a minute. And I have been told I have an excellent grasp of human anatomy." He hooked an arm around her and started her walking back toward the clinic fifth wheel.

She laughed. "No, you were told you were showing off your knowledge of human anatomy."

"I wouldn't show it off if it weren't excellent." He pulled

her hat off and dropped a kiss on the top of her head.

Peyton's heart soared. For the first time in her life she felt treasured for herself, not her family. Or her patched heart. Sure, Drew was a caretaker, but he also knew what it was like to lose someone he loved. He knew firsthand the heartbreak of loss. He would have never become so involved with her if there wasn't something about her that made the risk worth it. Right?

She allowed Drew to walk her to the clinic's side door and waited patiently for him to unlock and open the door. A roar from the crowd caught her attention. One of the girls must be having a good ride. Or a bad one. Sometimes, it was hard to read a rodeo crowd.

Drew reclaimed her attention by snagging her hand and pulling her into the clinic. Peyton paused, taking in the outdated but immaculately maintained equipment and fixtures. Drew was right. The clinic did need an upgrade. Trust her family to zero in on what someone needed most. But her cynicism was erased by Drew's clear pride in the clinic.

He patted the top of the exam table in the middle of the long, narrow space. "Bring that gorgeous anatomy of yours over here and let me grasp it." His blue eyes sparkled with amusement.

Regardless of how much Drew made her want to open herself up to him, the clinical setting brought back way too many memories.

Drew sobered. "I understand why you aren't a fan of anything remotely medical. Or doctors, for that matter."

She shook her head even though he'd accurately guessed what was bothering her. "Remember, you're not my doctor, Drew."

"I don't want to be your doctor, Peyton." He stepped close to her. "I want to be so, so much more. If you'll let me." He set her hat on the counter behind him and buried his hands in her hair. "I've spent so much of my life being afraid of losing the people I love. But in the short time that I've known you, you've shown me that loving, and really living, is worth the risk. To a point."

Peyton paused in the act of reaching for Drew's waist. Her heart stuttered. "To what point?" Her voice broke.

He dropped a quick kiss on her lips, but when he straightened, his expression was solemn. "I need to know that you understand how much your quest for thrills has the potential to cause pain to those who love you. Yes, I get that being smothered isn't any way to spend your life, and I would never do that to you. But you keeping everyone at arm's length and constantly taking risks for risk's sake is not cool either."

Despite having heard nearly the exact same thing from her family before, hearing them from Drew made them sink in. She realized she'd been manufacturing a sense of freedom by avoiding commitments and close relationships. But she wanted a close relationship with Drew.

Now, Peyton did grab Drew's waist. "I'd never want to cause you pain, Drew. Ever. I care about you too much." She couldn't bear the thought of causing him pain because she loved him.

A blond brow twitched upward. "You really do care about me?"

She gave him an exaggerated nod. "Yes. A lot."

"To the moon?"

She went up on her tippy toes and kissed his lips. "To the moon and back."

Drew dropped his forehead to Peyton's. "I love you, Peyton Halliday. Do you think that maybe we can find some middle ground between, say, BASE jumping and knitting by the fire?"

Peyton's heart exploded in the best way possible. She raised her hands from his waist to his gorgeous face and held him in place so he'd be sure to see how serious she was. "There is a ton of ground between those two things. And I can't wait to cover all of it with you, my Cowboy Doctor."

THE END

Want more? Check out Caitlin and Bodie's story in *The Bull Rider's Second Chance*!

Join Tule Publishing's newsletter for more great reads and weekly deals!

If you enjoyed *The Cowboy Doctor,*
you'll love the other books in....

THE RODEO ROMEOS SERIES

Book 1: *The Bull Rider's Second Chance*

Book 2: *Wrangling the Cowboy's Heart*

Book 3: *The Cowboy's Vow*

Book 4: *The Cowboy Doctor*

Available now at your favorite online retailer!

ABOUT THE AUTHOR

Having never met an unhappy ending she couldn't mentally "fix," Leah Vale believes writing romance novels is the perfect job for her. A Pacific Northwest native with a B.A. in Communications from the University of Washington, she lives in Central Oregon, with a huge golden retriever who thinks he's a lap dog. While having the chance to share her "happy endings from scratch" is a dream come true, dinner generally has to come premade from the store.

Thank you for reading

THE COWBOY DOCTOR

If you enjoyed this book, you can find more from all our great authors at TulePublishing.com, or from your favorite online retailer.

TULE
PUBLISHING

Made in the USA
Coppell, TX
09 August 2021

60209656R00135